FINDERS
KEEPERS

ALSO BY DAVID HOUSEWRIGHT

Holland Taylor Series

Penance
Practice to Deceive
Dearly Departed

Rushmore McKenzie Series

A Hard Ticket Home
Tin City
Pretty Girl Gone
Dead Boyfriends
Madman on a Drum
Jelly's Gold
The Taking of Libbie, SD
Highway 61
Curse of the Jade Lily

Written with Renée Valois

The Devil and the Diva

FINDERS KEEPERS

BY
DAVID HOUSEWRIGHT

Down and Out Books, LLC
3959 Van Dyke Rd, Ste. 265
Lutz, FL 33558
www.DownAndOutBooks.com

The characters and events in this book are fictitious. Any similarity to real persons, living or dead, is coincidental and not intended by the author.

Cover design by JT Lindroos

ISBN: 1937495396

ISBN-13: 978-1-937495-39-8

For Nicholas and Victoria

Acknowledgements

Special thanks to Kara Engler and Reneé Valois

PROLOGUE

About twenty people actually saw the robbery take place, although hundreds more would later brag that they saw it, too. James Richard McNulty was one of the twenty. He was sitting on a bench at the time, waiting for the bus that would take him home. He had come downtown directly after school to buy a birthday present for his mother. Not just any gift, either. It was a silver music box that played the George Gershwin song *Summertime* when you opened the lid, his mother's favorite tune. James Richard had to order the box special and the cost nearly exhausted his savings. Yet he decided it would be a small price to pay if the gift made his mother smile just once the bright, dazzling smile that used to fill him with such joy and comfort. Lately, James Richard's mother never smiled. There was trouble at home.

Sheila McNulty's husband, James Richard's father, had never been a happy man. Nothing pleased him; he shouted all the time. But in the last year his mood had grown increasingly worse. Even violent. He had been passed over for a promotion and in his anger and frustration; he blamed the failure on his wife and son. He claimed that being married and becoming a father had ruined his life. James Richard was tired of hearing it. He wished that his father would go away and his parents would get a divorce. Then it would be just him and his mother. He tightly gripped the bag that held the

1

music box and smiled at the thought.

James Richard glanced at his watch. It was nearly five P.M. The people who worked in the office towers that made up much of the city's downtown business district were just leaving their jobs or getting ready to. Already the sidewalks and city streets were clogged with pedestrians and cars; the air reverberated with the noise they made.

Where was the bus? James Richard wondered. He knew his father would yell even more than usual if he was late for dinner. He stood on the bench at the bus stop and searched the busy street. No bus.

James Richard sat down again as an armored truck drove past him and slowed to a stop in front of the large department store where he had purchased the music box. It was a no parking zone and the vehicle effectively blocked an entire lane of traffic. Drivers trapped behind the big truck leaned on their horns and cursed imaginatively. Still, the vehicle would not budge. Frustrated, the drivers were forced to wait until an opening could be found in the traffic and they were able to swing their cars into another lane.

Once the area behind the truck was clear of traffic, its rear door opened slowly, squeaking loudly on steel hinges. James Richard watched as two men dressed in uniforms that made them look like police officers, dropped to the ground and cautiously surveyed the scene around them. They both carried guns in black leather holsters. Seeing nothing to fear, they slammed the heavy door shut.

The taller of the two men rested his hand on the butt of his gun. The name Total Security was stitched to the pocket of his jacket and embossed on the badge above the visor of his hat. The other man, both younger and shorter than the first, carried a large, canvas sack that hung limp over his shoulder.

James Richard had seen armored trucks before. He knew they collected money from dozens of locations where a lot of cash changed hands—bank branches, jewelry stores, shopping centers, supermarkets—and transported it to a central bank where it would be safe from thieves. He hadn't thought much about them. Now, sitting at the bus stop and watching the guards, he wondered how much money the truck carried each day. Millions, he figured.

The two guards walked purposely toward the department store entrance. A man dressed in a suit and tie met them there. He glanced at his watch as the guards pushed through the glass doorway. Impulsively, James Richard looked at his watch, too. Five-oh-five P.M. Where was that bus?

It wasn't long before the guards stepped back outside the store. The taller man walked carefully toward the armored truck. He was clearing a path through the pedestrians for the younger man who was still carrying the large canvas bag over his shoulder. It was bulging and the guard seemed to labor under the load.

When the two guards reached the truck, the taller man rapped noisily on the back door. After a moment a third guard pushed it open and the younger guard heaved the bag onto the floor of the truck.

That's when the thieves hit.

James Richard didn't know where they came from; they seemed to appear out of thin air, two men wearing black ski masks that completely covered their heads and faces. They were carrying handguns.

"Put up your hands!" they shouted at the guards.

At first James Richard thought it was a joke, some elaborate gag. After all, tomorrow was April First—April Fool's Day! Only it wasn't a joke.

"Put up your hands!" the thieves shouted again, making it sound like they wouldn't say it a third time.

The guards hesitated. The one in the truck who had opened the door thought about reaching for his own gun, but one of the thieves was aiming his weapon right at him, so he raised his hands. James Richard nearly raised his hands too. The thieves were about thirty yards down the street and looking in the opposite direction. He moved toward them, although he couldn't explain why

Dozens of people on the sidewalk stopped and stared. They did nothing to stop the thieves.

A blue car raced past the bus stop and screeched to a halt directly behind the truck. The driver got out. He was also wearing a ski mask that hid his face.

The driver ran to the armored truck and climbed into the back while his partners watched the guards. Without hesitating, he pushed six canvas bags out the truck door onto the street. Each made a heavy thud when it hit the asphalt.

The driver dragged the bags across to his car and put them into the trunk. The bags all seemed heavy and it took two trips. Finally, he slid behind the steering wheel and sounded his horn.

One of the thieves shoved his handgun into the waistband of his pants and quickly climbed into the car seat next to the driver. The third thief walked slowly backward to the car, sweeping his gun from one guard to another and back again. The guards still had their hands up.

James Richard was close enough to hear the younger guard shout when the thief reached the open door of the car: "You'll never get away with it."

"What did you say?" the thief asked.

"You heard me."

The thief brought his gun up and trained on the center of the younger guard's chest. James Richard was sure he was going to shoot.

"No," he shouted. "Don't do that."

The thief turned toward the boy. Dark, clouded eyes stared at James Richard through the slits in the ski mask. He raised his gun and aimed it at the boy, freezing him in place. "You want some?" the thief asked.

James Richard didn't answer. All he could think of was that he would never see his mother smile again.

Somewhere a woman screamed, took a deep breath, and screamed again.

One of the thief's companions said something. Because of the screaming James Richard did not hear what it was, but it caused the thief to shout an obscenity at his partner. He gestured at James Richard with the gun, dismissing him as unimportant. He jumped into the back seat of the car. It was already racing down the street when the woman screamed a third time.

* * *

"Are you okay?" the policeman asked.

James Richard nodded although he didn't feel okay. Immediately after the thieves drove off, dozens of people began crowding around the armored truck and gawking at him and the guards. A dozen police officers arrived within minutes. An unneeded ambulance soon joined them. James Richard was leaning against the fender. Fear had caused him to throw up in the street and he was sure everyone had seen him and was laughing at him. The shame he felt was unbearable. There was more than shame gnawing at the boy's stomach though. There was an anger, an outrage, and a sadness, that he had not experienced before.

"He was going to shoot the guard," James Richard said.

"Yes," the officer answered.

"He was going to shoot me."

"Yes."

"What was wrong with him?"

The policeman set a large hand on James Richard's shoulder and gave it a reassuring squeeze. "Did you see anything?" he asked. He had introduced himself earlier as Sergeant Matt Rustovich, a member of the police department's major crimes unit. Rustovich was a big man and James Richard's first thought was that he played football or maybe basketball. Yet his eyes were gentle in a way that reminded him of his mother and his hand on his shoulder made the boy feel safe.

"I saw everything," James Richard admitted.

"Tell me what you saw."

James Richard inhaled deeply and told his story. He told it quickly so he wouldn't have to think too much about it. Sergeant Rustovich made him slow down and tell it again. And again. Making sure that no details were left out.

"What kind of car was it?" the officer asked.

"It was a four door, I remember that. It was blue. Sky blue I guess they call it."

The officer sighed and James Richard could tell he was disappointed. There were thirteen-year-olds who could tell you the make and model of every car ever built and all he could tell the officer was that the car was blue and had four doors.

"Did you happen to get the license plate number?"

James Richard shook his head. "It never occurred to me to look."

Sergeant Rustovich closed the notebook he had been writing in.

"Thanks for your help," he told the boy. Then he squeezed James Richard's shoulder again. "You should go home now."

James Richard thought that was a great idea.

* * *

The city bus left James Richard on a corner in the suburbs. The boy ran the two blocks to his home, knowing he was late, knowing he was going to get it when his father saw him.

He stopped just outside the front door and listened. He could hear voices coming from inside the house. Angry voices. The voices of his mother and father. He could not understand what they were saying. Did it matter? Lately, it seemed they didn't even know what they fighting over. Maybe it wasn't over anything. Maybe it was just an argument that started years ago and never stopped. He sighed and pushed open the door.

"Where have you been?" Simon McNulty wanted to know.

"I was downtown..." James Richard stammered.

"Do you know what time it is?"

"What happened was..." James Richard tried to say.

"Answer me!" the man demanded. "Do you know what time it is?"

"Leave the boy alone," Sheila McNulty said, coming to her son's defense.

"Shut up!" her husband shouted at her. To James Richard, "You think this house revolves around you, boy? You think we should all be waiting on you?"

"I was downtown..."

"What is that you have?" James Richard's father interrupted.

James Richard hid the bag he carried behind his back.

"It's for mom," he said. "For her birthday. I went downtown . . ."

"Give it to me."

"What?"

"Give. It. To. Me."

"No," James Richard protested. "It's for mom."

Simon McNulty grabbed his son's arm and pulled him forward.

"I tell you to do something, you do it!" he snapped.

He reached behind the boy, yanked the shopping bag from his hand, and pushed him backward. James Richard's heel caught in the carpet and he fell.

"Stop it!" Sheila McNulty shouted. "Leave him alone."

The man ignored her and tore open the bag.

"What is this?" he asked no one in particular, examining the silver box.

"It's a music box," James Richard answered from where he sprawled on the floor.

"You wasted your money on this?" his father asked contemptuously. "On this piece of junk? What a fool."

"It's beautiful," Sheila said.

"It's trash," he spat at her and smashed the box against the wall.

"No!" James Richard shouted and crawled quickly on hands and knees to the box. He picked it gently off the floor and cautiously lifted the lid, but the music wouldn't play.

ONE

Six Months Later

James Richard McNulty climbed the school bus steps, hesitating at the top.

"Take a seat," the bus driver said.

The seventh-grader paid no attention. He hung loosely to the pole next to the driver's seat as he scanned the faces of the other children. Some were looking out the windows. Some were reading. Some were talking to their friends. Still others were looking up to see which of their schoolmates the bus had stopped for.

"Where is she?" he wondered aloud, silently praying that she wasn't sick and staying home from school. *No,* he told himself, *she was never sick.*

"Take a seat," the driver repeated.

There. In the back. James Richard moved quickly down the aisle between the rows of bus seats. He stopped before a pretty girl with black hair cut short and eyes that changed from blue to deep green depending on how the light hit them.

"Lacey," he said, crowding next to her. "Let me copy your science homework."

"Whatever happened to, 'Good morning, Lacey. How are you today?'" she asked.

"I need it quick."

Lacey Mauer sighed quietly. A trick of the alphabet had placed her and James Richard McNulty side-by-side in nearly every line since kindergarten and a trick of the heart had made them friends. Lately James Richard had become such a pain though. Inconsiderate. Irresponsible. Rude. Ever since his mother divorced his father…

Something cold touched Lacey's heart and her whole body shivered. It seemed like the parents of half the children she knew these days were divorced and the idea it could happen to her own parents terrified her. She shook the painful possibility out of her head and reached inside her backpack. She removed a green folder and handed it to James Richard.

"Don't copy it word-for-word this time," she warned.

Without even a simple "thank you," James Richard opened the folder and began to transcribe the contents into a spiral notebook.

"Why didn't you do your own homework?" Lacey asked.

"I forgot," James Richard replied, which was his excuse for everything these days.

"Did you at least study for the Spanish test?" she asked.

James Richard stopped writing. His head jerked up abruptly.

"Spanish test?"

Lacey shook her head sadly.

James Richard closed his eyes and bowed his head.

"I forgot," he said.

* * *

"Lacey," James Richard whispered. "C'mon Lace."

The girl ignored him. He wanted her to slide over in her desk chair so he could get a good look at her test paper. She refused. Other people might think that letting James Richard steal her answers during a Spanish exam was no different than letting him copy her homework, but Lacey figured there was a fine line between the two and no way was she going to cross it.

James Richard shifted his weight in his own chair and tried to look around Lacey's shoulders. When that failed, he glanced at the papers of the kids sitting on both sides of him, trying hard not to turn his head. Unfortunately, the boy on his right was leaning on his elbow while he wrote, effectively hiding his paper and the girl on his left wasn't doing any better than he was.

James Richard looked down at the white sheet of paper in front of him. He tapped his Number Two pencil against his lower teeth. He not only didn't know the answers, he didn't even understand the questions. He glanced at the large clock that hung above the classroom door. Twenty minutes left. Panic caused little beads of sweat to form on his forehead.

"Lacey," James Richard whispered again.

Suddenly a hand fell flat on his test paper, making a loud, slapping sound. The unexpected noise made James Richard flinch. He glanced up quickly, meeting the eyes of Mrs. Spanier. Just as quickly he looked away.

Mrs. Spanier's fingers slowly crumbled the test paper into a ball. "See me after class," she said.

James Richard nodded. He slumped down in his chair. His head lowered until his chin rested against his chest.

* * *

"Make me understand," Mrs. Spanier said quietly. The bell had sounded; the other kids had all filed off to their next class. Only James Richard remained behind, standing in front of his teacher's desk, afraid to look at her face. "I want to understand," she added.

James Richard said nothing. A trickle of sweat ran down his back and he absentmindedly fingered the initials SRL stitched on the left breast pocket of his knit uniform shirt—short-hand for St. Rose of Lima. He swore he could hear the ticking of the big clock above the door, but maybe that was just his heart pounding.

"Look at me!" Mrs. Spanier shouted.

James Richard looked. Mrs. Spanier was not an attractive woman, certainly not as attractive as his mother. She always wore a pleasant expression though and her eyes twinkled in a way that made her students want to confide in her. Until now. Now her lips were a thin, straight line and her eyes were narrow slits that contained nothing but fury.

"What's going on with you, young man?"

"Nothing," James Richard answered too quickly.

"Nothing?"

"Nothing," James Richard repeated, his voice rising. "I was cheating and you caught me. Now you can expel me or do whatever else you want."

Mrs. Spanier leaned forward, rubbing her hands together in a way that made James Richard think that she was the one who was afraid.

"This is not like you," she told him. "I know your record and I know you. You're a straight-A student. Last year you were named Student of the Quarter."

James Richard nodded. He would have received the honor twice except Lacey Mauer beat him out in the Spring.

"More important than that, you're a good kid."

James Richard didn't know what to say to that. He dropped his head and studied his feet.

"I want your parents to come in and see me tomorrow night," Mrs. Spanier said at last.

Fear pounded James Richard in the stomach.

"No," he said, shaking his head.

"I think so."

"No, you... You don't understand," the boy stammered.

"Understand what?"

"My mother…"

"Yes?"

"She… she works."

"At night?"

"Yes."

"Your father, then."

"No. He…"

"He what?"

"He doesn't live with us anymore."

Mrs. Spanier leaned back in her chair and sighed as if she was listening to a story she had heard many times before.

"He left us," James Richard added.

"I understand," Mrs. Spanier said.

* * *

It was because she understood that Mrs. Spanier insisted on meeting James Richard's mother the following evening at the school; his mother had to take an unpaid day off from work and she wasn't happy about it. James Richard sat on a chair outside the door to Mrs. Spanier's classroom while the two adults spoke privately. They spoke for a long time. Or maybe it only seemed like a long time to James Richard because they were talking about him.

He muttered a word he wouldn't have dared to speak in front of his mother, then looked up and down the hallway of the exclusive private school to make sure no one else had heard him either. When he was sure the corridor was deserted, he said the word again. It was a word James Richard's father had used many times.

* * *

When the end came, it came quickly. Just three days after his father smashed the silver music box against the wall, he punched James Richard's mother, knocking her against the same wall. The next day, while he was away at work, Sheila McNulty had all the locks in the house changed and contacted an attorney. Instead of being outraged as Sheila and James Richard predicted, Simon McNulty seemed amused. He said he'd be happy to give Sheila a divorce. He even smiled when he said it—the first time James Richard could remember seeing his father smile. He agreed to pay the alimony and child support that Sheila requested and to an equal division of their property. He even agreed to *give* his wife and son his share of the heavily mortgaged 13-room house they owned in the suburbs. Because of his cooperation, the divorce was settled within a month. Less than a week later, Sheila and James Richard discovered why Simon McNulty had been so generous—he had stolen most of their savings and fled the state. There would be no alimony payments. No child support. As far as Simon McNulty was concerned, his wife and son ceased to exist.

"To hell with him," James Richard said at the time.

His mother smiled weakly and stroked his cheek and said, "Don't curse, dear."

James Richard didn't miss his father. What was there to miss? The shouting? The insults? Simon McNulty had never been kind to him, even when he was a baby. He never played with him, never took him to baseball games or to the park—he was always too busy, even when busy meant doing nothing more than sitting in front of the TV. He never showed any interest in James Richard's grades, which were usually spectacular. In fact, it was because he and his son didn't get along that James Richard's grades were so good; the boy spent most of his time studying in his room or at the library so he could avoid his father.

Now, just six months after his father left, James Richard couldn't recall a single conversation they had together that lasted more than a minute. In most of those his father merely listed his expectations: "I expect you to cut the grass, I expect you to clean the garage, I expect you to take out the recyclables."

No, James Richard did not miss his father. But he sorely missed his mother whom he hardly saw now.

Sheila McNulty had told James Richard that everything would be fine following the divorce and he believed her; he was nearly giddy with joy when it was finally over. Only the pleasure he felt was soon replaced with a feeling of desperation. The problem was money.

Mrs. McNulty worked as an accountant for a company that owned a chain of restaurants. She made a good income, but not good enough to pay for their huge house in the suburbs all by herself. Or the new car she drove. Or expensive clothes. Or tickets to the opera and the ballet. Or the hefty tuition for St. Rose of Lima, the private elementary school James Richard attended. But Mrs. McNulty insisted that her son was going to have all the advantages he enjoyed before the divorce—when they were living on two incomes. To pay for it she took a second job. She became the night manager for one of the restaurants her company owned. As a result, James Richard never saw his mother accept on weekday mornings while she prepared for her daytime job and he readied himself for school. She was home on weekends, but most of that time was devoted to washing clothes, cleaning the house, shopping for groceries, or other household chores.

At first it had actually been fun; James Richard had never enjoyed such freedom. He came and went as he pleased, without telling anyone where he was going or when he'd be back. If he wanted a snack before dinner, he had a snack before dinner. If he wanted a snack *for* dinner, who was there to say no? He'd crank the volume on his music until the windows rattled and no one nagged that it was too loud. Bedtime was when his spirit moved him, which was usually late.

All that changed as the days turned to weeks and the weeks turned to months. James Richard became increasingly bored with his freedom. Because he could now do whatever he felt like, James Richard suddenly didn't feel like doing anything.

In the beginning, he spent a lot of time with Lacey Mauer, especially in the summer, walking or riding his bike four blocks down and three blocks over to her large brick house across from the nature preserve. Only she always wanted to play in the preserve or shoot baskets or access the new computer program she was into or talk about school or a book she had read and he didn't want to do any of those things. Nothing seemed to hold his interest for more than a few minutes at a time now. Certainly not his homework, which he did on the school bus or not at all.

More and more James Richard found himself home alone, sitting in the dark each night in his father's old chair, watching TV programs he was too young to see. Instead of becoming excited by it, the nightly phone call from his mother annoyed him. He no longer filled his mother's entire dinner hour with highlights from his day. Now when she asked, he was just "okay" and he was always doing "nothin'."

Now this.

James Richard knew that at St. Rose, the penalty for cheating was automatic and immediate expulsion and he had mixed feelings about that. On one hand, he was horrified. Leaving the school where he had done so well in the past, leaving his friends, leaving Lacey—the thought hit him so hard he nearly lost his breath. Plus, he worried what people would think of him. James Richard McNulty was not a cheat!

On the other hand, he would probably be forced to transfer to the public school. The *free* public school. Which meant his mother wouldn't need to work so hard to pay for his tuition, uniforms, books, computer fees. She could quit her night job and stay home with him!

At least, that was as far as James Richard's thinking took him before the door to the classroom clicked open and his mother stepped out.

* * *

"Thank you again," she said to Mrs. Spanier.

James Richard looked up from his chair as his mother closed the classroom door. She had always been a pretty woman, tall and slim, with corn-blonde hair and eyes the color of chocolate. Yet he didn't appreciate how pretty until one day last year following basketball practice when the college kid who coached the team stared at her in awe and gushed, "Wow, mothers sure have changed since I was a kid." Only lately she was looking old. Even her bright yellow hair seemed to have lost its shine. She seldom smiled.

Sheila McNulty knelt next to her son and with one hand, brushed the hair off his forehead. James Richard's eyes burned with tears, but he refused to let them fall.

"Mrs. Spanier is giving you an F on the test, but she's not reporting you for cheating," Mrs. McNulty told her son softly.

James Richard nodded. He didn't know what to say.

"If it happens again, they'll expel you."

He nodded again.

"Promise me…"

"I promise, Mom," James Richard said.

"I realize this is my fault…"

17

"No," Richard said abruptly.

"I need to spend more time…"

"No," Richard said again. "It's my fault. I've been lazy, I've been goofing off, I've been…"

Mrs. McNulty pressed two fingers against James Richard's lips and shook her head slowly.

"We'll both try to do better," she said.

"Yes," James Richard said. "Yes."

"Give me a hug," Mrs. McNulty told him.

"Why?" James Richard asked.

"Because we both need one," she told him.

James Richard wrapped his arms around his mother and squeezed tight. The tears finally fell, hot and wet, against his cheeks.

TWO

Three men in their early twenties sat together in a booth and spoke in whispers, their heads almost touching as they leaned toward each other across the table. The bar was noisy. Country music blared from a jukebox and the laughter and shouts from a victorious bowling team added to the tumult. Still they were careful to keep their voices low and when the waitress brought beers to the table, they stopped speaking and sat back while she served them. As soon as she departed, they leaned forward again and were back at it.

"Are you sure, Sickler?"

"Yeah," said Sickler. "I'm sure. The man in Canada said he'd pay us seven hundred thousand dollars in cash."

"American money, right? Not Canadian?"

"American money," Sickler assured him with a contemptuous smile. What did Truax think, that he was as stupid as him?

"It's all set," Sickler continued. "We take the four hundred and sixty-eight thousand dollars we stole from the armor truck and buy eighteen kilos of cocaine with it. We then take the eighteen kilos of cocaine to Canada and sell it for seven hundred thousand dollars."

"That's a profit of two hundred and thirty thousand dollars," the man named Worlie announced. "For each of us."

"Two hundred and *thirty-three*," Sickler corrected him.

Truax rubbed the palms of his hands together.

"That's the kind of arithmetic I like."

"So do I," Worlie added.

"More important," said Sickler. "We can spend it. We won't need to be afraid the cops can trace it back to the armor truck job."

"Yeah," said Truax.

"Yeah," he repeated, pounding a drum roll on the table top with his fists.

"I'm tired of waiting," said Worlie. "It's been six months since we stole that money and I want to start spending it."

"You know the first thing I'm going to buy?" asked Truax. "I'm going to buy a sportscar. A Jaguar. I'm going to buy…"

"Shut-up about what you're going to buy," Sickler hissed. "Haven't you guys learned anything yet?"

"I was only saying…"

"I know what you were saying," said Sickler. "I don't want to hear it. Look, we robbed that truck six months ago and we've been sitting on that money ever since, not spending any of it. Why?"

No one answered.

"Why?" Sickler insisted.

"Because the money could have been marked," said Worlie, looking down at the table. "The cops might have been able to trace the money using serial numbers."

"That's right," Sickler agreed. "Now we have a chance to get out from under that. What do you think is going to happen though if we start throwing it around, huh? What do you think is going to happen if all of a sudden we start buying expensive sports cars and stuff? We have records, all three of us. We've all done time for armed robbery. If we start throwing around a lot of money, what do you think the cops are going to say?"

Again his partners hesitated to answer.

"What do you think they're going to say?" Sickler repeated.

"They're going to say we stole it," Worlie muttered.

"That's right," Sickler said. "Use your heads."

"Yeah?" said Worlie. "Were you using your head when you were about to shoot the guard?" Anger, like lightning, flashed across Sickler's face and his hands knotted into fists. "What about the kid at the bus stop? You were going to shoot him, too."

"I don't like people talking back to me." Sickler pointed a finger in Worlie's face. "That includes you."

The words sent a chill down Worlie's spine.

Sickler was smiling now as he reached for his beer. His smile held no warmth or humor and it frightened Worlie. In fact, everything about Sickler frightened him. The two men had met in prison. They had been confined to the same cell. Sickler was bigger than Worlie by half a foot and about thirty pounds. And there was a kind of hatred in his eyes; a hatred for all things life had to offer. Two minutes after he walked into the cell, Sickler had smiled the same joyless smile and told Worlie, "Let's get the rules straight."

"What rules?" Worlie had asked.

"Do what I tell ya or I'll kick your teeth in," Sickler had answered, still smiling.

"Oh, those rules," Worlie had said.

He attempted to put up a brave front, but in the end, Worlie did everything Sickler told him to do. He was afraid not to. Even when Sickler recruited him for the armored truck robbery, called him up and said, "I got a job for ya," Worlie was too frightened to say no.

Now he was involved in armed robbery.

How did this happen? Worlie wondered. How did he get mixed up with these low-life thieves? The answer came to him easily, and painfully, as he signaled for another beer. It was because he was a low-life thief.

"I'm just saying," Worlie said. "*We* all have to be smart."

"Yeah? Let's talk about smart," said Sickler. "Let's talk about that jewelry store. You pull on your mask, pull out your gun, walk in and make the salesclerk give you the cash. No jewels, just cash. How much? Twenty-five hundred?"

"Twenty-eight."

"Twenty-eight hundred bucks you get holding up that jewelry story, waving your gun around. When you're outside, the mask off, getting into your car, you see this old man standin' right there in front of you with his mouth hanging open, watching. You could've shot him right then. Put him away and you outta there clean, ain't nobody gonna catch you. But you don't shoot him. Why? Because you're a nice guy and there are things a nice guy won't do. So, what happens? The old man ID's your vehicle, picks you out of a line-up and you end up doing forty-six months in state prison. Is that smart?"

Worlie didn't answer.

"Not me pal," Sickler continued. "Listen to what I'm telling you. If there's a man standing in front of me, if it's between me going to prison or him getting killed, there's nothing to think about, man, I'm takin' him out."

"Yeah, yeah, yeah," Truax said. "You're a real tough guy. Tough as nails. I came here to talk business. We going to talk business or what?"

Lightning again flashed across Sickler's face. He had met Truax in prison, too. He was about Worlie's size—five-ten, one hundred and eighty pounds. Only, unlike Worlie, Truax didn't scare. Not one little bit. Worse, he had a big mouth, always telling people what to do, always trying to take over. Sickler hated Truax. Which was fine with Truax because he hated Sickler. The way Truax figured it, in a couple of days this entire affair

22

would be safely over. Then he could rip off Sickler's ears and shove them down his throat, no problem.

"Your guy in Canada is all lined up?" Truax asked Sickler.

"All lined up," Sickler said. "We give 'em the junk, he gives us the money. If you want, we can divvy it up right there and then go our separate ways."

"Sounds good to me," Worlie said.

"If we can trust your guy," Sickler told Worlie.

"We can trust him," Worlie vowed. "We bring him the money Thursday night, the day after tomorrow, he gives us the cocaine. We can be halfway to Canada before dawn."

"If we can trust him," Sickler repeated, his voice low and harsh with lips curled up over his teeth like a wolf about to pounce.

I want this to be over, Worlie thought but didn't say.

THREE

Lacey Mauer's father stirred the rich, red spaghetti sauce simmering in a pot on the front burner of the kitchen stove. He glanced at the digital clock on the microwave. It was four-forty-five Wednesday afternoon. *Supper in an hour*, he figured.

Behind him his daughter and James Richard talked basketball. He wondered where he had gone wrong. He had been born and raised in northern Minnesota. Hockey was his passion and he tried to instill it in his daughter. He spoke eloquently about the joy of skating on ice, of slap-shots and crisp, solid body checks. He described the deeds of legendary players like Bobby Orr, Gordy Howe and The Great Gretzky. But she just stared like she felt sorry for him.

"Here," Mr. Mauer said, scooping a wooden spoonful of sauce from the Dutch oven. "Taste this."

He brought the spoon to Lacey, his free hand cupped beneath it to catch any drops. She was still dressed in her school uniform—a red and blue plaid jumper and white shirt—and sitting on the countertop next to the sink, her legs dangling over the edge. She sipped at the spoon and made a face.

"Too much oregano," she said.

Mr. Mauer stared at her for a good three seconds and said, "Get off the counter."

She got.

"There is no such thing as too much oregano." He brought the spoon to James Richard. "Taste this."

James Richard did as he was told.

"Hmm, absolutely perfect," he said. "The best spaghetti sauce I've ever tasted."

"You're welcome to stay for dinner," Mr. Mauer told him.

"Thank you, sir."

"It'll be nice to have someone at the table with good taste," he added as he frowned at his daughter. "Too much oregano," he muttered under his breath as he turned back to the stove.

"I thought cooking was women's work," James Richard said. "Least, that's what my dad always said."

"You ever cook for yourself, James?" Mr. Mauer asked. "Make a sandwich, scramble an egg?"

"Sure."

"Ever feel like putting on a dress?"

"No."

"Exactly."

"Huh?"

"Work belongs to whoever is doing it," Mr. Mauer replied. "It's women's work when women are doing it and it's men's work when men are doing it. "

"It's person's work," Lacey added.

"Sounds funny, but yeah," Mr. Mauer replied. "I cook because I enjoy it and because I'm good at it and because I'm a teacher and Lacey's mother is a lawyer and I get home before she does. It makes sense that I cook."

"Do you do housework, too?" James Richard wanted to know.

"Sure."

"He doesn't do laundry," Lacey said. "At least not anymore. He destroyed half of Mom's wardrobe one time and she revoked his washer and dryer privileges."

"It wasn't half," Mr. Mauer corrected her. "Closer to a third."

James Richard wasn't listening. His mind had slipped

away for a moment and he started thinking about the things he could be doing, should be doing around the house to help his mother. Wash clothes? He could wash clothes, he told himself.

"I notice you don't do much laundry," Mr. Mauer told his daughter. "Or even clean up your room with any regularity."

In reply, Lacey cupped a hand around her right ear.

"Wait. Do you hear that?"

"What?" Mr. Mauer replied.

"Do you hear that?" she asked James Richard.

He shook his head, puzzled.

"Something outside," Lacey said. "It's calling us. It's saying, 'James, Lacey, come out and play'."

Mr. Mauer smiled and shook his head. He was used to his daughter's tactics.

"We'll be in the preserve," Lacey announced and headed for the door.

Lacey's father was tempted to stop his daughter. It would be night soon and the idea of Lacey wandering the woods after dark always made him nervous. He quickly dismissed the fear. Lacey had grown up across the street from the nature preserve. She knew it the way most children knew their own backyards. The numerous man-made trails that cut through the woods and the boardwalks that provided dry passage over the swamps were second nature to her. So were the many natural passages that the park keepers knew nothing about. Lacey could map every lake, every pond, every stream and creek. She knew where the beavers built their dams and the raccoons made their dens and the egrets laid their eggs. She was on a first name basis with many of them. If someone became lost in the Theodore Roosevelt Nature Preserve, it wouldn't be his daughter. More than likely the authorities would beg Lacey to lead the search. So Mr. Mauer gave them a vague idea when supper would be ready and waved them on their way.

"If at all possible, don't get your uniforms dirty," he said.

* * *

Winter was coming slowly. Halloween was only two weeks off, yet the temperatures hovered in the low seventies and most of the countless oak, elm, birch, ash, chestnut, poplar, willow and fir trees that populated the sprawling nature preserve were still resplendent with autumn leaves of almost unimaginable colors.

James Richard and Lacey hiked through the woodland without jackets or sweaters. Lacey led the way. She wanted to review the progress "K. G." the beaver, had made on his new lodge.

"Why K. G.?" James Richard had asked.

"Kevin Garnett, National Basketball Association MVP 2004."

"Oh."

Lacey led James Richard off the beaten path and through a stand of poplar and birch trees. They dodged shaggy bushes and low-hanging branches for about one hundred yards until they came to a clearing that overlooked a large pond. A hump of small logs were piled with great care at the far end of the pond, but K. G. was nowhere to be seen. The two seventh graders decided to wait. They were silent. Alone. A gentle breeze stirred the branches of trees but beyond that there was no sound.

Lacey was suddenly aware of James Richard's presence in a way she had not known before. His blond hair, brown eyes, narrow nose, his hand supporting his weight as he leaned against the trunk of a birch tree, his height—at least four inches taller than her. It was like she was noticing these features for the first time. Her heart began a fretful pounding. She recognized it immediately as fear. Fear of the words in her heart that she simply could not make herself speak.

They had been friends. Friends in the truest sense of the word, sharing their deepest secrets and their greatest fears. Their history stretched back to kindergarten, to the beginning of time. It included St. Rose and basketball and summer camp and even this place, this pond, these woods. Yet lately Lacey had been thinking of James Richard in a way that confused her. In her thoughts, she had been adding the word "boy" to the word "friend."

She did not know why she was doing this, although she could tell you when it began. It began after James Richard's parents divorced and he started becoming increasingly depressed and lonely over his mother's absence. When it looked like Lacey's "boyfriend" would be expelled from school, her fear brought tears to her eyes and she tossed and turned in bed all night and well into the morning. She had never done that before.

Lacey moved closer to the water so James Richard couldn't see her face. She touched her lips with two fingers. She had kissed him once. Last year. Only at the time, she hadn't really felt it.

She had been teased by two bully boys on the bus, upperclassmen who should have known better. Muchlinski and Landeen were their names, a couple of Jean-Claude Van Damme wannabee's whose exaggerated grunts and imaginative—if highly inaccurate—karate kicks might have been mildly amusing if they weren't always directed at kids half their age and size. They were mocking Lacey's new, short hairstyle.

"She wants to be a boy," they laughed at her.

"Why not? She looks like one."

James Richard had come to her defense. Sort of.

"Better leave her alone," he told the older boys. "If

she gets mad, she'll beat you up and the whole school will know it. You don't want the world to know you got beat up by a girl, do you?"

The two boys hesitated for a moment, regarding Lacey carefully. Both of them were a year older, a full head taller and at least forty pounds heavier. They broke out laughing. James Richard shrugged.

"I tried to help," he told Lacey.

After the bus stopped at school and the children trooped off, Lacey turned to face the older boys, moving into an American Free Fighting Stance, her feet at forty-five-degree angles and a shoulder's width apart, knees slightly bent, weight distributed evenly on each leg, her hands in a guard position, ready to strike or block. When they saw the way Lacey stood, Muchlinski and Landeen laughed at her.

"Look Landy. She thinks she's the Pink Ranger," Muchlinski mocked.

"No, the Red Ranger," Landeen laughed, referring to the Pink Ranger's male counterpart.

"You two watch the *Mighty Morphin Power Rangers*?" Lacey asked. "At your age? Really? How mature of you."

Muchlinski and Landeen knew when they were being mocked and they didn't like it. So, they did a foolish thing. They tried to lay hands on her. It took Lacey approximately 15 seconds to teach them the error of their ways.

Lacey had studied karate two days a week, every week, for five years. Her mother had insisted that she learn how to defend herself, and although Lacey had resisted the idea at first, fearful that people would make fun of her, she came to like it very much and as with most things, she excelled at it. Muchlinski and Landeen could testify to the fact as they lay writhing on the ground in pain. James Richard hovered above them.

"I warned you," he told them.

Lacey was breathing hard and her whole body seemed to quiver, more from excitement that exertion.

"A lot of help you were," she said between breaths.

James Richard draped his arm around her shoulders in a brotherly embrace and said, "I'm proud of you. No one in this school will ever bother you again. Or me, either, 'cause I'm your friend."

Lacey stopped breathing all together. Without thinking she went up on her toes, leaned in and kissed his mouth. It wasn't much of a kiss. Little more than a peck, really. She hadn't thought much about it. Until now. Now she touched her lips with her fingertips and wished she had it to do over again.

After the fight, Lacey had been afraid that James Richard would shy away from her. She thought he might be reluctant to spend time with a girl who was a better fighter than he was. Instead they grew even closer. For a time, James Richard called her "Sally," after Sally Kimball, the tougher than algebra fifth-grader who punched out Bugs Meany in the Encyclopedia Brown books.

"You don't call me Sally anymore," Lacey reminded James Richard from the edge of the pond.

"Huh? Why would I call you that?"

Lacey was astonished. *Don't tell me he's forgotten already?* Then, *No, no, James Richard is only pretending he forgot. He doesn't want to show his feelings.* Boys are like that, Lacey knew. At least that was what she had always been told.

"I'm glad they're not throwing you out of school," she whispered.

"Me, too."

"I would..." Lacey hesitated, decided to go for it. She took a deep breath and said, "I like you. I really like you. Do you know what I mean?"

"Sure," James Richard replied. "I like you, too."

Only he didn't know what she meant. Lacey could tell by the way he continued to stare across the pond at the beaver lodge, searching for K. G.

The pounding in her heart slowly faded. She felt—and looked—like she was about to cry.

James Richard came *this close* to hugging her. Only he couldn't muster up enough courage.

Of course I like her, he told himself. He couldn't think of anyone he liked more. She knew that, didn't she? He had said it. He had said *"I like you, too."* What else could he say? Maybe he could tell her she was pretty. Maybe he could tell her that the way her eyes changed color from blue to green made his heart flitter-flop. But it all sounded so lame in his head that he couldn't imagine actually speaking the words out loud. Besides, she would just think he was dumb.

"Basketball sign-up is tomorrow after school, boys and girls teams," James Richard said.

"Yes, I know," Lacey replied. She sighed audibly, added, "You going out?"

"I guess."

"Guard?"

"Uh huh. You?"

"Sure?"

"Same position as last year?"

"Yeah. Guard. Maybe some forward."

"Uh huh," James Richard said.

Lacey sighed again.

"C'mon," she said. "Let's go home. I know a short cut."

* * *

Worlie sat in bed in his dingy eight-foot-by-ten motel room reading the Help Wanted Ads in the back of the newspaper. He wondered if it wasn't about time he quit being a thief and got himself a *real* job. His old man was a welder; he did all right. His uncle was a machinist. He made a pretty good living, too. Neither of them were afraid that one day the cops would come and take them to prison for the rest of their lives.

'Course, his take after the drug swap in Canada would amount to nearly a quarter of a million bucks. It would take his old man and his uncle four, maybe five years to make that kind of money—and they'd have to pay taxes on it!

'Course, if Worlie got caught…

There were several want ads for welders and machinists and plumbers, too. Worlie ignored them. He had never been good with his hands. He was so smart, he had dropped out of high school. Later, while he was in prison on the jewelry store rap, he earned his general equivalency diploma. But what kind of job could he get with a crummy GED? Not much if you wanted better than slinging burgers and schlepping fries at some fast food joint.

Still, it was a start, wasn't it? he told himself. He could get a job in a fast food joint, maybe become a manager someday. Hey, with his share of the money, he could buy his own restaurant. Wouldn't that be something? A business owner. He would stop stealing. Maybe get married and raise a family, raise good kids who wouldn't be stupid like him. The more Worlie thought about it, the better he liked the idea.

"I'll go straight," he announced to the walls and ceiling. "Right after this last job."

* * *

James Richard read the note again:

I hope you had a good day in school. I love you. We'll do something special together this weekend. No TV or computer tonight, okay? Remember to do your homework.

Love Mom

"Sure," he muttered.

Nothing had changed, James Richard decided. All the talking they had done the previous evening, stuff about how things were going to get better—it was just talk. He was still alone in this mausoleum of a house. He was still communicating with his mother through notes and text messages or over the telephone.

James Richard sighed heavily, dropping the note on the floor; he didn't even bother to look where it landed. He grabbed a bag of potato chips from the cupboard and a can of cola from the refrigerator and brought them both into the family room and turned on the TV and his PC. He ate and drank while watching an R-rated film about a guy who hacked up beautiful, young women with a meat cleaver while surfing his Facebook page. He wondered vaguely why the villain never attacked ugly, old woman. He'd have to ask his mother about that—over the weekend.

FOUR

About four dozen kids—boys on one side of the basketball court, girls on the other—were dressed in gym clothes and shooting baskets even though it wasn't an official practice. Johnny Barczak moved among the boys, a clipboard and pen in his hands. He knew most of the kids from previous tryouts. Still, he dutifully wrote down each player's name, although he had already pretty much decided who would probably make the team. Like Tommy Glaser. Five-eleven and only thirteen years old.

When he came to James Richard McNulty, he paused. "I need this kid," he told himself as he wrote down James Richard's name. "How many thirteen-year-olds can put up a three-pointer with any consistency? Who could pass? Who could run the floor?"

Barczak was excited. He could see his future unfold before him. With McNulty and Glaser playing in tandem, Barczak could win the conference championship, maybe even the districts, maybe even state. Why not? When he graduated from college in the with his Phys Ed degree, he could use his success to leverage a coaching job in a high school. Then move up to college. Then the pros. There was only one problem.

"Walk with me," he told the youngster over the rumble of basketballs dribbled on the wood court.

James Richard followed his coach to the bleachers at the far side of the gym.

"Lookit here," Barczak said. "I can't believe I'm having this conversation with you of all people."

"What?" James Richard wanted to know.

"Your grades, man."

"What about 'em?"

"Here's the thing," Barczak said. "The season starts in four weeks. Grades for the first quarter are out in three. If you don't have at least a 2.5 grade point average, the school won't let you play no matter how good of a jump shot you have. Right now, this here paper," Barczak showed James Richard a green sheet with the St. Rose letterhead printed on top, "says you don't have the numbers. Hear what I'm saying?"

"I didn't know that, about the grades, I mean," James Richard said.

"That's because up until now, you've never had to worry about it. Look, they're not AWFUL. Maybe we can talk to your teachers."

The idea of sitting out the season, academically ineligible they'd mark on his chart, startled James Richard. As with everything else in his life these days, he had been indifferent about making the basketball team. Only once he held the ball in his hands, dribbled it, banked it off the glass, a kind of electricity began to surge through his body. He had become excited at the prospect of a new season—a new beginning—and he hadn't been excited about anything for a long time. He wouldn't let it go, he decided. He couldn't.

"I'll get my grades up," he promised. He almost added, "carve it in stone," but he didn't.

"Can you?" Barczak asked.

"Don't worry, Coach," James Richard assured him. "I'm not that far behind. I can make it up."

For a brief moment James Richard wondered if he could. He didn't have the three weeks Coach Barczak supposed. Finals would be given in two weeks, right before Halloween, with grades coming out a week later. Could he improve a grade point average in two weeks that he had been trashing for two months?

Yes, James Richard declared to himself, dismissing all doubt from him mind. He would do it. He had to do it. He needed basketball. It was all he had left.

"I hope so," Coach Barczak said. "Partly because I know you like to play. Mostly though, I'll be honest here, with your outside shooting and with Tommy Glaser in the middle, man, we can be deadly this year. It'd be like John Stockton and Karl Malone."

"Who?"

Barczak looked at the expression on the thirteen-year-old's face. *What is it with kids today?* he wondered. *Didn't they study history?*

"Never mind," he said.

* * *

The public library was across the street and half a block down from St. Rose and the two institutions sponsored many programs together. The library informally stored St. Rose texts, computer programs and other materials for students to study after school hours. The librarian knew James Richard and was happy to see him sitting in his old, familiar spot at the table across from the door and near the floor-to-ceiling windows. He hadn't been around much lately. She called to him softly, only he didn't hear. He was wearing headphones and listening to a Spanish language tape played on computer while scrolling through Spanish-English transcriptions on the screen. She moved to his side and tapped his shoulder. Startled, he removed the headphones.

"We close in fifteen minutes," she warned him, pointing at the clock above the door. It was a quarter to nine. James Richard nodded his thanks and replaced the headphones over his ears.

His mother would not approve of him staying so long at the library. It meant taking a city bus to get home, for one thing. Yet James Richard felt he would get more work done here than at his home, where he would be distracted by TV and video games and Facebook and all the rest. Besides, since she now worked nights and couldn't pick him up, he'd have to take the bus home after basketball practice anyway. What was the difference if he left at five-thirty or nine?

Later, while he stood at the bus stop three blocks north of his school, James Richard realized that there was a big difference. For one thing, it was dark. For another, he was alone. At five-thirty the bus stop attracted a lot of other kids who were going home from school and grown-ups returning from their jobs. Then there was the ride itself. James Richard would be traveling all the way from the southern suburbs through the heart of the city and into the northern suburbs. The bus ride would take nearly an hour. Well, at least he'd be able to get some more studying in, he decided.

"Only two weeks left," he reminded himself as the lights of the bus approached.

* * *

The sound of squealing brakes followed by a car horn startled James Richard, forcing him to look up from his American history textbook. The bus was on University Avenue now, a major thoroughfare that cut the city in half. It was lined with retail shops of all kinds: pizza joints, auto parts stores, fast food restaurants and bars. Dozens of people walked the sidewalks. When James Richard looked up, he saw a man dressed in dark clothes running toward the bus. He was carrying a large suitcase above his head with both hands and yelling something. The bus slowed and stopped in the middle of the block as the man ran in front of it. Its front doors swished opened. The man carrying the suitcase climbed on board. He was breathing hard and his face was pale from running. He spoke earnestly with the driver as he fished in his pocket for money. He seemed relieved when he discovered the correct change.

The bus driver hit the accelerator and the bus jerked forward. The man with the suitcase nearly fell as he made his way past James Richard to the back of the bus. Upon reaching it, he slid the suitcase on the seat, but he did not sit down. Instead he stood, watching something outside the back window. James Richard looked through the side window. He saw two men trying to cut across the busy street, but on-coming traffic forced them back to the curb. One of them bent over and rested his hands on his knees and if he was exhausted from running a long, long, way. The second man was gesturing wildly at the bus. The driver didn't see him though and kept the vehicle moving down the avenue.

James Richard glanced over his shoulder at the man now sitting on the back seat of the bus. He was clutching the handle to the suitcase with both hands and smiling.

James Richard shrugged and went back to his textbook.

* * *

"Oh no! No! No! No!"

A half dozen passengers, including James Richard, turned in their seats to look at the man with the suitcase. Only about five minutes had passed since he had boarded the bus. He was standing again and looking out the back window.

"Now what am I going to do?" he asked himself

aloud.

James Richard looked out the side window. There was a car coming up fast behind the bus, but he couldn't make it out.

"Nuts," the man with the suitcase said loudly. "Nuts! Nuts! Nuts! Nuts! Nuts!"

James Richard returned to the window. The car in the next lane had overtaken the bus and was now matching its speed. The vehicle was sky blue and had four doors. James Richard told himself he had seen it before, but couldn't remember where. Inside the car were three men, two in the front seat and one in the back. The man sitting on the passenger side of the front seat was pointing a finger at the back of the bus. He then drew it slowly across his throat, moving the finger from ear to ear. He seemed to be laughing.

James Richard glanced back at the man with the suitcase. He was also watching the car and holding his throat with both hands as if he had just been cut there. He seemed even more pale than before.

James Richard looked for the car again. It was speeding past the bus. All he could see were its taillights. He went back to his history text.

* * *

James Richard heard a low scraping sound behind him that he couldn't recognize. He glanced over his shoulder. The man with the suitcase had abandoned the back seat. He was now sitting across the aisle from James Richard, two rows back. The suitcase was standing upright in the aisle next to him. It reminded the boy of one his mother owned. He didn't linger over it. He was studying a chapter on the Spanish-American War—Teddy Roosevelt was about to lead his Rough Riders up San Juan Hill and he wanted to learn how it turned out. The scraping noise distracted him again. Only this time when James Richard looked, he discovered that the man was now sitting directly behind him. He had crossed the aisle, dragging the suitcase with him. His face had turned a ghastly white and his breathing was irregular. At first James Richard figured the man was sick. Then he realized that he was scared. That made James Richard scared, too.

The man with the suitcase paid no attention to James Richard. He didn't even seem to notice he was sitting there. Instead, he stared straight ahead without expression. When the bus slowed and stopped, his eyes grew wide and the corners of his lips turned downward. He looked like he was in pain.

The bus doors swished open and a man climbed the three front steps. He ignored the fare box and turned toward the back of the bus. He studied the faces of each passenger until he found one he recognized crouched down in the seat directly behind a blond kid maybe twelve or thirteen in a private school uniform, SRL stitched over his heart. The man smiled and when he did, the man with the suitcase gasped. That made James Richard gasp, too, although he couldn't tell you why. The man who had just boarded the bus had sandy-blond hair and blue eyes and didn't look frightening at all.

"Hey, buddy," the bus driver said. "Forget something?"

The sandy-haired man glanced at the driver who was pointing to the fare box.

"Correct change, please," the driver said.

James Richard heard a scraping noise behind him.

The sandy-haired man scowled like he didn't appreciate the interruption and dug deep in the pocket of his blue jeans for money.

The man with the suitcase hopped up.

The sandy-haired man, attracted by the sudden

movement, turned toward him.

The man left the suitcase and dashed to the back door of the bus and hit it hard with his shoulder. The door gave and he squeezed through.

The sandy-haired man cursed. The bus lurched forward as the driver pulled away from the curb, knocking his passenger off balance. The sandy-haired man cursed again.

"Let me off, let me off!" he screamed at the bus driver. The bus driver was happy to oblige, but took his own sweet time about it. The sandy-haired man dashed out the door and began chasing the other man.

James Richard watched it all from where he was kneeling on his seat. All of a sudden the Battle of San Juan Hill didn't seem that interesting.

* * *

James Richard was still kneeling on the seat and looking through the windows when once again the bus began accelerating away from the curb. Someone yelled, "Hey!" and the driver pounded his brakes. The bus jerked forward violently and rocked backward. The abrupt movement threw James Richard from his perch. He hit the back of the seat in front of him and fell to the floor. A heavy object slid into him, banging his head. It was the suitcase that belonged to the man who had jumped off the bus.

"Everyone all right?" the bus driver called. The passengers murmured adjectives concerning the state of their health. Everyone was more or less intact.

"How 'bout you kid? You all right?"

The bus driver was looking in his mirror at the reflection of James Richard rubbing his head.

"Yeah," said James Richard. He climbed to his feet and righted the suitcase, setting it next to his seat.

"Sorry about that, folks," the bus driver called over his shoulder. "Some jerk in a blue car pulled out in front of me without signaling."

James Richard rubbed his head some more and stared angrily at the suitcase. His mom was right. Riding the city bus *was* the pits.

* * *

The name of the street changed from University to Lincoln Parkway as the bus left the city limits and entered the northern suburbs. It drove three miles without a halt until James Richard pulled the cord, signaling the driver with a low *ting* that his stop was approaching.

James Richard was standing in the back doorway as the bus slowed. He couldn't wait to get off.

"Don't forget your suitcase," the driver called to him.

"What?"

"Your suitcase."

"That's not my..."

"Take the suitcase," the bus driver insisted, yelling at the boy.

James Richard hesitated.

"C'mon kid, I gotta schedule to keep."

James Richard flinched at the words and grabbed the suitcase by the handle. It was heavy and he half-carried, half-dragged it out of the bus. As he set it on the ground, the big vehicle shuddered and pulled away from the stop. James Richard looked after it.

"It's not my suitcase," he finally found the voice to say.

The taillights of the bus became dimmer and dimmer until they disappeared altogether. James Richard kicked the suitcase.

"What am I supposed to do with you?" he wondered

out loud.

He kicked the suitcase again.

Finally, the boy grabbed the handle and began carrying-dragging it to his house. Normally, the trip would have taken five minutes tops, however, between the suitcase and his book-laden backpack, James Richard was moving a lot of weight and the job took him fifteen minutes. When he reached his front door, he kicked the suitcase again.

"I sure hope I get a reward for this," he declared.

The first thing James Richard did after unlocking the door with a key he wore on a chain around his neck, was dash to the bathroom. The second thing he did was drag the suitcase into the kitchen. He attempted to heave it up on the table, but decided it wasn't worth the effort. He left it on the floor.

James Richard went to the refrigerator, found a root beer and pulled its top. He drank thirstily while he regarded the suitcase. Should he open it? It was private property after all. But how else was he going to learn the identity of the owner and return it? There were no outside tags, nothing with a name on it. The heck with it, he decided and set the root beer on the table. He pushed the suitcase on its side and snapped open the locks. He lifted the lid slowly.

His ears filled with a loud rushing sound like air escaping from a leaking automobile tire. He swallowed hard and the sound stopped. He blinked his eyes once, twice, three times, closed them for a few seconds, opened them again. He reached out and gently touched the green bills before pulling his hand back, afraid his fingers would be burned.

The suitcase was filled with money.

James Richard began picking up packets of bills. One, then another, and another until he couldn't hold anymore.

"My God," he said in a whisper. "It's real."

* * *

Three men stood before the dispatcher at the bus depot.

"You're in luck," the dispatcher told them. "Bus 115 is pulling in just now. If you left your suitcase aboard, it's probably still there."

Only it wasn't. The bus driver told the three men that nothing was left on his bus. He even let them look for themselves.

"Somebody must have taken it," said the man with sandy-blond hair and blue eyes.

The bus driver looked at him like he had seen him before but couldn't place where.

"I don't know who," the driver said at last. "There was a fella... Naw, he didn't take anything when he jumped off. Hey, wait a minute. Now I remember. A kid. Got off in the suburbs, about a mile from the nature preserve. Had a school uniform on. He was carrying a suitcase. Big sucker. Almost forgot it. I had to remind him."

Without so much as a "thank you," the other two men each took an arm of the third and pulled him away from the bus driver. The sandy-haired man protested, but the others didn't care.

"This is really making me angry," said the one named Sickler.

"You and me both," said Truax.

"It's not my fault," said Worlie.

"You said your guy was trustworthy!" Sickler was shouting now. "This guy. This Fast Eddie. You said he could be trusted to sell us the cocaine. Only what happens? The man tries to sell us powdered sugar, instead. Powdered sugar! Looks like cocaine but it ain't!

Then he steals our money and runs—this Fast Eddie you think is so trustworthy. We end up chasing him all the way across town."

"It's not my fault," Worlie insisted.

"Whose fault is it?" Truax wanted to know. When Worlie didn't answer, Truax said, "Eddie didn't have the suitcase when he got off the bus."

"The kid's got it," Sickler said.

"This kid who took the suitcase, do you remember him?"

Worlie closed his eyes, tried to see the boy in his mind's eye.

"What about it?" asked Sickler.

"Do you remember him?" Truax asked again.

Worlie opened his eyes. He almost wished he couldn't remember, but the picture was clear in is mind. He said, "Blond kid maybe twelve or thirteen in a private school uniform, SRL stitched over his heart."

FIVE

The police station was crowded and noisy with people bustling back and forth, all of them looking like they were late for something and James Richard wondered if it was always like that. From where he and his mother sat on a bench against the wall, it reminded him of an airport except he was the only one with a suitcase.

James Richard was working on only three hours of sleep, yet he never felt more awake. All his senses were revved up. Adrenaline surged through his body like water in a faucet; he could see and hear everything. The snatches of conversation he picked up fascinated him, especially one exchange between two police officers who walked past him and his mother.

"We found him at the county fairgrounds. Name 'a Fast Eddie."

"What is it with crooks and nicknames?"

"He was pretty beat up, couple of broken bones. He'll be in the hospital for a month."

"Who's catching?"

"Rustovich got the call."

"He has all the fun."

James Richard looked at his mother, who also heard the conversation. She shook her head sadly and said nothing.

They sat on the bench for another twenty minutes with Mrs. McNulty growing more and more impatient. She was looking at her watch for about the fiftieth time when a man dressed in blue jeans, a white shirt and a black sports jacket walked into the station house. He saw Mrs. McNulty, couldn't miss her sparkling blonde hair and her chocolate ice cream eyes. He smiled. James Richard saw the smile. He didn't like it. Men were always smiling at his mother and he wished they would stop.

"Hey, Matt," the desk sergeant called out to the man
"Yeah?" he answered.

He went to the police sergeant who was sitting behind a large desk on top of a high platform in the center of the room. The police sergeant spoke to him quietly and motioned toward the McNulty's. The man smiled and came toward them like he couldn't think of doing anything he enjoyed more.

"Can I help you?" Rustovich asked Sheila McNulty, still smiling.

"I don't know, can you?" she answered in a way that let the policeman know that she had been smiled at before.

"I'm Detective Sergeant Matt Rustovich with the major crimes unit," the man answered and offered his hand. Sheila shook it. The man completely ignored James Richard. He said, "The desk sergeant mentioned something about a suitcase."

Sheila McNulty frowned, debated how to answer. While she hesitated, James Richard answered pointedly, "I found a suitcase on the bus last night." Sergeant Rustovich looked at him like he was seeing the boy for the first time. "We're here to turn it in."

James Richard didn't want to turn it in, God knows. He argued with his mother about it most of the night. She was adamant though and when James Richard at last forced himself into a crying jag in an attempt to get his way, she simply sent him to bed with the promise that they would take the money to the police station before school the next morning.

"You found a suitcase on the bus?" Sergeant Rustovich repeated.

"Yes," James Richard said. He nearly added, "sir" to his answer, but saw no reason to be respectful to this man who kept smiling at his mom.

"That's not a police matter," Rustovich said. "You should have taken it to the bus company's lost and found."

"There's something in it," James Richard said.

Rustovich hesitated for a moment, then smiled once again on Sheila McNulty.

"Well, why don't we take a look," he said. "Where is the suitcase?"

"The desk sergeant has it," Mrs. McNulty answered.

Together, the three of them crossed over to the desk sergeant's platform. Rustovich grabbed it by the handle. "Heavy," he said, surprised by the weight. He carried it back to the bench and set it on top.

"Did you open it?" he asked Mrs. McNulty.

"Of course," Sheila answered, waiting to see the detective's reaction.

"Find anything of value?" Rustovich asked, working the latches.

Mrs. McNulty shrugged.

Rustovich opened the suitcase and looked inside.

"Wow," Rustovich said, drawing out the word.

"Four hundred and sixty-eight thousand dollars," James Richard said. "We counted it last night. It took hours."

"Wwwoooooowwwwww," Rustovich repeated.

"Funny, that's just what I said," Sheila McNulty told him.

* * *

Five minutes later Shelia and James Richard McNulty

49

were sitting in comfortable chairs in a conference room on the third floor of the police building. Shelia had been served coffee, no cream one sugar. James Richard was given orange juice although he preferred root beer. He was also eating a chocolate-covered donut with sprinkles. Mrs. McNulty had declined the offer of bakery.

"Tell me what happened," Detective Rustovich said. James Richard related his story six times, forgetting and adding details with each telling. Finally, on the seventh try, he mentioned the county fairgrounds.

"What?" asked Detective Rustovich.

"That's where the guy got off and the other guy started chasing him."

"At the county fairgrounds."

"Well, near there," said James Richard.

Rustovich paused for a moment, thinking. Then he was on his feet.

"I'll be right back," he said. "There's something I want you to look at."

He was heading for the door of the conference room.

"Can I use the restroom?" James Richard called after him.

"Sure."

* * *

When he returned, Detective Rustovich showed James Richard a plastic sleeve holding two rows of three photographs each. He called it a "photo array" and asked James Richard to select the photo of the man who left the suitcase on the bus. James Richard chose the middle photo in the bottom row.

"Are you sure?" Rustovich asked.

"Yes, sir," James Richard replied. "This is the guy."

"Look again," Rustovich urged.

James Richard looked again.

"And?"

"It's still him."

Rustovich nodded.

"Okay," he said.

"Is that Fast Eddie?" James Richard asked.

Rustovich was surprised the boy knew the name and showed it. "What do you know about Eddie Meeks?" he asked the boy.

"I heard two officers talking," James Richard replied. "They said a guy named Fast Eddie was beat up at the county fairgrounds last night, put in the hospital. I didn't know his name was Meeks."

"Edward Meeks. He made his living selling phony drugs to teenagers and other people who didn't know any better. He would fill small plastic bags with powdered sugar or crushed antacid tablets and pretend it was cocaine. By the time his customers figured it out, Eddie was gone. That's how he got his nickname. Fast Eddie. The way Eddie figured it, he was doing the community a service, keeping bad guys from buying drugs. I busted him for it, but the judge threw the case out. He said with so many creeps out there selling the real thing, he wasn't going to waste the court's time with a guy like Eddie. Can't say I blame him. This time though it looks like Fast Eddie tried to rip-off the wrong folks this time. They worked him over pretty good."

"The guys chasing the bus?" James Richard asked.

"That's my guess. We found Eddie's car in the parking lot of an old, abandoned factory on the Eastside. His trunk was open. Inside his trunk was a suitcase. Inside the suitcase was sixteen kilos of powdered sugar. Next to his trunk, on the ground, was two more kilos, the bags broken open and sugar scattered everywhere. Eddie is pretending he doesn't know anything about it."

"Drugs." The word was spoken softly by Sheila McNulty.

"Don't be alarmed," Rustovich told her, but she ignored him.

"My son is involved in drugs?"

"No, no, not at all," Rustovich said. "It's just an unhappy coincidence."

"Coincidence?" Sheila McNulty didn't believe that for a minute.

"Excuse me," Rustovich told her. "I'll return in a moment."

Rustovich left the conference room. Sheila McNulty turned toward her son. "Drugs?"

James Richard asked, "Do you think they'll let us keep the money?"

Mrs. McNulty shook her head. She wanted no part of the money. As far as she was concerned, this whole situation was just getting worse and worse.

* * *

Sheila McNulty had called both James Richard's school and her office to report that they would be late. She wished she had told them, "really, really late." She was now on her fourth cup of coffee while James Richard was finishing his third donut. Finally, the door to the conference room opened again. A man in a blue police uniform with silver bars on the points of his shirt collar swaggered in with Detective Rustovich trailing behind.

"Hi," the officer said, extending his hand. "I'm Lieutenant Michael Kennedy. I have good news." He shook both Sheila's and James Richard's hand before adding, "You can keep the money."

"What?" James Richard said. He was on his feet now.

"I don't understand," said Mrs. McNulty. She looked at Rustovich. He was leaning against the wall, his arms folded across his chest. He refused to speak and the way he worked his jaw muscles, she knew something was bothering him.

"Finders keepers, losers weepers," recited the lieutenant.

"That's what I said," James Richard told him.

"I don't understand," Mrs. McNulty repeated.

"I just spoke to the city attorney," the Lieutenant added. "I told him that there was absolutely no way we can identify the owner of the money. He agrees the money now belongs to you."

"What about the man on the bus?" Mrs. McNulty wanted to know. "What's his name?"

"Fast Eddie," said James Richard.

"He claims it's not his," Kennedy assured him. "He has said so many times."

"But," Mrs. McNulty said.

"We have no way of identifying the owner of the money," Kennedy said, interrupting the woman. "So now it's yours. Congratulations."

"Yes!" James Richard shouted, pumping his fist.

"There is one thing though," Kennedy said. "And you don't have to do this if you don't want to. There's no statue, no law that says you have to."

"What?" asked Mrs. McNulty.

"Just to be fair to the real owner we'd like to keep the money for a week. We'd like to put a story in the paper that says a large amount of money was found and if the owner can identify it, he or she should claim it."

"How is that fair?" James Richard wanted to know, suddenly fearful that the treasure was slipping from his grasp.

"James Richard!" Mrs. McNulty snapped.

"If someone does claim it, we'll make sure they

actually do own it before we give it out," Kennedy assured the boy. "We'll make sure they describe the suitcase in detail and that they know the exact amount of money it contains."

"That's perfectly fair and reasonable," Mrs. McNulty said.

"Ahh, Ma," said James Richard.

"Cheer up," said Lieutenant Kennedy. "In seven days, you'll probably be rich."

James Richard sure liked the sound of that.

"It'll be fun for me, too," Kennedy added. "I'll be able to give you the money the day before I retire."

"You're retiring?" asked Mrs. McNulty.

"A week from tomorrow it'll be thirty years I've worked as a police officer."

"That's nice," Mrs. McNulty said, still confused.

Sergeant Rustovich left the room.

* * *

"This is so great, this is so cool," James Richard kept repeating as his mother drove him to school.

"It's not our money, James Richard," his mother told him.

"So?"

"So we need to find the rightful owner, even if the police don't."

James Richard was shocked.

"Are you serious?"

"It's not our money."

"You don't get it, do you?" James Richard accused his mother. "You don't understand anything at all."

He kicked the dashboard hard with his foot.

"James Richard!" his mother snapped at him. "I will not tolerate this behavior."

"You just don't know anything!"

"I know that you think you're going to go out and buy a lot of..."

"I am not!" James Richard shouted. "I'm not thinking about buying anything. Gawd!"

He kicked the dashboard again.

"Fine," Mrs. McNulty said. She pulled the car to the curb; stepped too heavily on the brake. The car lurched forward and stopped. She turned to James Richard.

"Fine," she said again. "You explain it to me. Tell me why we must keep money that doesn't belong to us?"

"The money... It means you won't have to work two jobs anymore," James Richard blurted, anguish in his voice. "It means you can stay home. It means we can be a family again."

The words cut deeply into Sheila McNulty's heart. She backed away from her son until her spine was hard against the car door.

We can be a family again.

"Is that what it means?" Sheila McNulty asked, her voice suddenly low, almost a whisper.

We can be a family again.

Tears welled-up in Sheila McNulty's eyes as she listened to James Richard. He seemed to have it all figured out, even if she did not.

"We can put the money in income-producing investments," he said. "We learned about this in school. You invest the money and take the dividends as income. That way you have money coming in to pay the bills, but you're not spending the principal."

"I understand how it works," Mrs. McNulty told him gently.

"You can stay home without losing income," he added. "It's perfect."

Mrs. McNulty was silent for a long time. She had been wrong, she knew. All the time since the divorce she had worked two jobs to earn enough money to buy things for her son. A big house, nice clothes, a decent school, but it wasn't things he had needed. It was love. Supervision. It was having someone to depend on, someone who would always be there, things money can't buy. How ironic, she thought, that it took a suitcase full of money to teach her that.

She brushed the tears from her eyes and said, "I know we have problems that we need to work out. Only money isn't the answer."

"It sure looks like it to me," James Richard insisted.

* * *

If not for the numerous cars parked around it, St. Rose of Lima grade school would have looked deserted. Worlie watched the building through binoculars from the front seat of Truax's Ford Escort parked two blocks down. Nothing moved. All the children were inside.

"This is impossible," he muttered.

Sickler whacked Worlie's head with the butt of his handgun.

"You had better hope to God it's not impossible."

Truax, sitting behind the steering wheel, said, "St. Rose of Lima. It's the only school in the phone book with the initials SRL. They have red and blue uniforms, too. The kid goes here. He has to."

"All you need to do is pick him out," Sickler said.

"I don't know if I can," Worlie confessed. "I only saw him for a second."

"Pick him out," said Truax. "We grab him, make his parents give up the money. Simple."

Add kidnapping to my growing list of sins, Worlie told himself silently. He was becoming less and less of a nice guy every day.

SIX

Lacey Mauer's squeal was loud and piercing and every kid within eighty feet turned to look at her. The thirteen-year-old was hopping up and down on her chair and muttering "Ohmigod, ohmigod" over and over. She squealed some more and the kids wondered what her story was.

James Richard noticed the other kids watching and pulled his head in like a turtle.

"Shhhhh," he cautioned the girl.

"I don't believe it!" she shouted.

"Keep it down, wouldya," James Richard told her. "I don't want the entire cafeteria to hear."

Lacey's voice dropped to an earnest whisper.

"That's why you were late for school," she said.

"Uh huh."

"Ohmigod, ohmigod," she yelled, back to full volume now.

Miss Hoedeman, the science teacher, who had drawn lunchroom duty that day, abandoned her post near the door and came forward.

"You win the lottery, Mauer?" she asked.

"No ma'am. But James Richard did," Lacey replied much too loudly. Several kids who heard her did a double take and started murmuring. The teacher nodded. Being a practitioner of the art, she knew sarcasm when she heard it.

"Then McNulty should be screaming, not you," she told the girl.

"Yes, ma'am."

"Mr. McNulty," Miss Hoedeman added. "Remember. Money can't buy happiness or a good grade in the science test Monday."

James Richard smiled knowingly, as if he understood so much more than his teacher and for a moment Miss Hoedeman thought, maybe he *did* win the lottery.

Miss Hoedeman strolled back to the cafeteria door, her arms crossed over her chest. In the short time it took her to get there, the noise in the cafeteria had changed dramatically. The usual upbeat clatter of kids at lunch was replaced by a sound that was dull and hushed, like traffic from a long way off. It sounded to Hoedeman like four hundred children all decided to whisper at the same time. She noticed that many of the children were now sitting very close together as they engaged in earnest conversations.

"They're restless," she told herself. She wondered if it was caused by the unseasonably warm weather or the approach of finals or simply because it was Friday. There seemed to be a lot of whispering and not much eating going on. Hoedeman was tempted to eavesdrop, but convinced herself that it would be an unfair invasion of privacy.

James Richard ate his lasagna. He didn't like it. He found it much too dry for his taste. He wolfed it down anyway. He was very nervous and eating gave him something to do with his hands. Lacey Mauer, on the other hand, was far too jazzed to eat.

"Nearly half of a million dollars," she repeated at various levels of volume. Her words were picked up and tossed across the cafeteria by the other children one table at a time.

"A half a million."

"A million."

"Ten million."

"What are you going to do with it?" Lacey asked.

"Give it to my mom to invest," James Richard replied, his mouth full.

"Not all of it?"

James Richard nodded and explained his plan.

"You have to keep some for yourself," she urged. "You have to buy something. You have to go to Disney World."

"To visit some dumb rodent that hasn't made a movie in my lifetime, I don't think so," James Richard said. He added, "I wouldn't mind a new smartphone."

"I know a place where you can get a deal," Lacey said. "Course, you don't need a deal anymore."

James Richard smiled. He and Lacey bussed their trays, Lacey's was still half full, and left the cafeteria for the playground beyond the doors where Miss Hoedeman stood.

"Mom wants to keep a low profile," James Richard confessed to his friend. "She's afraid we might attract all kinds of ding-a-lings. So you have to promise not to tell anyone."

Lacey said, "I can keep a secret."

They nodded to Miss Hoedeman and slipped through the door. Voices buzzed behind them.

"Did you hear? McNulty won like thirty million dollars in the lottery."

"Really?"

"If I had that much money, I'd quit school."

"If I had that much money, I'd buy the school."

* * *

It didn't take long before James Richard realized his secret was out. By fifth period it seemed half the student body had made some comment to him about the money. Most of the kids merely told him what a lucky pup he was. Some asked him what he was going to do with it all. While estimates ranged from one million to fifty million dollars, no one had the amount correct.

To his surprise, some of his classmates seemed angry with him. They acted like James Richard had somehow stolen the money from them while others accused him of turning into a jerk overnight. One of his classmates even told him, "*You think you're better than the rest of us.*"

At first James Richard tried to be honest with everyone.

It's less than half a million dollars.

I didn't win it or steal it, I found it.

I'm giving it all to my mom.

No, I don't think I'm better than you. Why would you say that?

Only his answers seemed to please no one and James Richard became frustrated, angry and confused. He wondered why his classmates were treating him so weirdly. He wondered if he was at fault. What did you do? He found some money on a bus and turned it in. What's the matter with that? He could think of only one person to talk to.

He met Miss Spanier after final period. She seemed genuinely pleased by his good fortune. Yet she was even more delighted that he spoke to her in Spanish. For his part, James Richard didn't know why he was speaking Spanish. He just slipped into it, perhaps because the entire situation seemed so foreign to him.

"*No sé qué hace,*" he said, admitting he didn't know what to do.

"*Todo el mundo está emocionado,*" Miss Spanier replied, telling him that everyone was excited. "*En algunos días se olvidarán de todo. Dale tiemp.*" It'll pass in a few days. Give it time.

"*Lo que molesta es la gente que está enojada, la gente que me trata como un idiota.*" What gets me are the kids who are angry, who treat me like a jerk.

"Todos ellos quieren ser como rú." They all wish to be you.

"¿Lo crees?" You think?

"Si."

In English, James Richard asked, "You don't think the money will change me, do you? I heard money changes people."

"I guess sometimes it does," said Miss Spanier. "You're a pretty smart guy though. I don't think it'll change you. At least I hope it won't. I like you just the way you are."

Miss Spanier's words both startled James Richard and ignited a small fire in his belly that warmed him all over. He felt it spread to his face and he turned away, afraid she would see him blush.

"Gracias," he said and left her classroom.

* * *

Something happened to James Richard on the basketball court that he could not explain. Everything that had happened to him over the past twenty-four hours, all thoughts of money and murdered drug dealers, faded to black. There was only him and the ball and his teammates.

Johnny Barczak couldn't help but notice it. James Richard ran practice drills like he invented them. His passes were crisp and always on target. During the fifteen minute scrimmage, he blocked three shots from three separate opponents; all of them taller than he was including Tommy Glaser. He scored twelve points. In fifteen minutes! His shooting was amazing. He simply could not miss.

"They call it being in a zone," Barczak told him later. "You were in a zone."

"I never felt like that before," James Richard

admitted. "It was like I wasn't even playing. It was like I was watching someone else play who looked like me."

"Neat feeling, huh?"

James Richard nodded, a broad grin on his face. "You think that's the way LeBron James feels sometimes, when he's putting up those fifty-point games?"

"Exactly like that," Barczak told him.

"That is so cool."

"How 'bout your grades?" his coach asked guardedly. "Are you in a zone there, too?"

"You bet." James Richard's smile was broad and bright. He felt like he had the world in his pocket.

"Hit the showers," Barczak told him and James Richard hurried away. He hesitated only when he heard his coach's voice.

"Can I help you?" James Richard turned to see a man with short brown hair leaning against the bleachers at the far end of the gymnasium. "Hey buddy, can I help you?" Barczak repeated.

The man hurriedly left the gymnasium without replying, but not before giving James Richard a long, hard stare.

"McNulty?" the coach asked. "Ever see that guy before?" James Richard shook his head. "Let me know if you see 'em again."

"Sure," said James Richard.

* * *

Lacey Mauer spoke so loudly, James Richard had to hold the cellphone away from his ear. He was sitting at his kitchen table, a can of root beer in front of him.

"I still can't get over it," she told her friend.

"Will you forget about the money. Geez."

"I can't help it, it's just so exciting."

"It's only money."

"Yeah, right."

"Well, maybe it is important."

"I'll say."

"Only it's not going to help me pass geography."

"Who cares?"

"I care," James Richard said. "If I don't ace the final and get my grades up, they're gonna toss me off the basketball team. That's why I called. I need your notes."

"Say, did you hear?" Lacey asked, changing the subject. "The girls' team is going to scrimmage the boys before the season opener. Me and you pal," Lacey added, her voice suddenly sounding like an announcer at a professional wrestling match. "In your face, disgrace basketball. Loser leaves town forever and forever is a long, long time."

Lacey said more, something about her size six-and-a-half tennis shoe and James Richard's sorry behind, only James Richard wasn't listening. A loud thump captured his attention. It sounded like something large bouncing off the side of his house. He listened intently, heard nothing more.

"Huh, what did you say?" he asked.

"I said, 'I'm going to fast-break you into the floor'," Lacey repeated.

"Talk is cheap," James Richard reminded his friend. "If you..."

There it was again.

"If I what?"

"Shhhh, I heard something."

"What?"

"Hang on."

James Richard gently carried the phone with him as he crept silently to the front door and turned on the light. He looked carefully through the spy hole, but saw nothing. He went to the windows. The street was empty and quiet. He then went to the back door after first turning on the garage and porch lights. He saw nothing. Nothing moved. He returned to the telephone.

"What was it?" Lacey wanted to know.

"Nothing," said James Richard. "It must have been the wind."

"The wind's not blowing," Lacey told him.

SEVEN

Sickler paced Worlie's tiny motel room, moving restlessly to the bathroom and back again, then retracing his steps. While he walked he kept practicing his quick draw, reaching under his jacket, pulling out his gun and squeezing the trigger, listening to the "click" as the hammer fell on an empty chamber.

"Stop doing that," Truax told him. "Sit down."

Sickler ignored him.

"I said sit down!" Truax shouted, balling up the newspaper and tossing it across the room. "You're driving us nuts."

"I'm driving you nuts? I'm driving you nuts? Huh? Is that what you said?"

Sickler drew on Truax and pulled the trigger.

Click.

"You are nuts," Sickler announced.

"It's over," Worlie said bitterly, his dreams of buying a fast food restaurant shattered. He was sitting next to Truax and like Truax he had reread the newspaper article several times before Truax crumpled it up. "It's over," he repeated.

Sickler pulled his gun yet again and aimed it at Worlie's forehead. "It's not over until I say it's over," he shouted.

"Put that away," Truax said. Instead, Sickler turned and pointed the gun at him. Truax smiled, reached under his jacket and drew his own gun. He made sure Sickler got a good look at it. Then he said, "Mine's loaded."

Sickler had nothing to say to that.

"You want to listen to me now?" Truax asked. "Or should I do the world a favor and blow your brains out?"

From where Worlie was sitting, a thin layer of fear-induced sweat on his forehead and under his arms, doing the world a favor seemed like a good idea.

"I'm listening," Sickler said. His voice was calm and well-modulated. He wasn't fooling anybody though. Both Truax and Worlie could see the rage behind his eyes.

"What was our original plan? We were going to snatch the kid and force his parents to turn over the money," Truax asked and answered his own question.

"Only according to the newspaper, the parents haven't got the money," Sickler said.

"According to the newspaper, they will in a week," Truax reminded him.

"If the rightful owners don't claim it."

"Why, you big dummy," Truax spat at him. "We're the rightful owners."

"If we don't claim it..." Worlie muttered.

"Duh," grunted Truax.

"The cops'll give the money back to the kid and his family and then we can go for it," Sickler said.

"Gosh, you're smart," Truax mocked him.

Sickler put his hand in his pocket and fingered the loose bullets he found there. *One of these days*, he told himself while he stared at Truax. *One of these days.*

Truax smiled at Sickler as if he could read his mind.

"The day the cops return the money, we snatch the kid," Truax said.

"If we don't kill each other first," Worlie added.

* * *

Lieutenant Kennedy was in his living room watching Cartoon Network while eating a bowl of Cap'n Crunch cereal. He used to watch Saturday morning cartoons with his kids when they were young. While they grew out of them—grew up and moved out, in fact—he couldn't break the habit.

The phone rang. It was Sergeant Rustovich.

"You saw the article in the newspaper, Lieutenant?"

"Yeah, I saw it."

"I still say this is a bad idea."

"Has Fast Eddie talked, yet?"

"No."

"Is he going to?"

"No."

"Then we keep doing what we're doing."

"These are bad people," Rustovich said.

"I know," said Kennedy.

"It makes me worry about the kid and his mother even more."

"Me, too."

* * *

Laundry, grocery shopping, house cleaning, Sheila McNulty decided all that could wait. She vowed to spend the entire weekend with her son. She even prepared a long list of activities the two could enjoy together. James Richard thought most of them were pretty lame. Apple orchard? Who wants to go to an apple orchard? The idea of spending time with his mother so delighted him though that they could have gone to the dentist for all he cared.

As it turned out the apple orchard was a lot of fun. James Richard and his mother were met at the entrance by the owner's wife. Her name was Agnes, that's what it said on the name tag pinned to her sweater, and she insisted James Richard make his own apple juice. He resisted at first, but gave in at his mother's urging. With Agnes' help, he chopped up a few apples and placed them into the well of an apple press. Turning the crank, he crushed them into pulp. A stream of juice flowed from a small hole in the base of the press into a small, metal pitcher.

"Very good," Sheila McNulty said after drinking half a cup.

"Very, very good," James Richard agreed, eyeing the apple press. "We should buy one of these."

Mrs. McNulty looked heavenward and shook her head.

"All aboard," a voice happily shouted. The voice belonged to the owner of the orchard, his name tag said Peter. He was sitting at the controls of a small tractor. Attached to the tractor was a long, low-slung wagon loaded with hay and two dozen passengers. Sheila McNulty and her son quickly bought two plastic bags with string handles, six-fifty each James Richard noted, and hopped on the wagon just as Peter started it in motion. A pretty woman and her teenage daughter began singing as the wagon lurched forward, *Return To Pooh Corner,* in perfect, two-part harmony. The riders applauded wildly when they finished. The woman's husband started to sing in a terrible baritone. *"Since my baby left me..."* The audience shouted him down to his mock astonishment and raucous laughter.

The tractor pulled the hay wagon along a narrow, rutted dirt road that traversed the sprawling orchard. At strategic points it would stop and Peter would call out varieties of apples: Mackintosh, Heralson, Redwell. At each stop, a few passengers would disembark and commence filling their bags. Others, waiting at the stop, their bags overflowing, would climb aboard the wagon for the return trip to the entrance.

James Richard and his mother jumped off the wagon when Peter yelled, "Sweet Sixteen." Soft red and specked with yellow, Sweet Sixteens were smaller than most apples, just the right size for snacks, James Richard concluded. He filled half his bag with low hanging apples before deciding the best, most juicy apples were at the top of the trees. With his mother repeating "be careful" every few minutes, he climbed a tree and started picking.

"Young man, could you throw down those over there?" asked an older woman, someone's grandmother, James Richard figured, pointing to a branch just within James Richard's reach.

"Sure."

As it turned out, she *was* somebody's grandmother. She had come to the orchard with her husband in search of ripe, juicy apples fit for her family's tenth reunion. Her brothers, sisters, children, grandchildren, nieces, nephews and cousins were gathering from all over the country. She preferred Sweet Sixteens for her applesauce because of the way they mixed with sugar and simmered in the pan, although for apple pie, you just couldn't beat Cortlands, she claimed.

"Why?" asked Mrs. McNulty, who was thinking she hadn't baked a pie since forever.

The grandmother looked at the younger woman without blinking for a full fifteen seconds before replying, "Because that's what my grandmother used and she should know. She brought the recipe over from the old country after the war with the Spaniards..."

Spanish-American War. 1898. "Remember the Maine!" Fought primarily in Cuba and Manila Bay, Philippines. U.S. gained the Philippine Islands, Guam and Puerto Rico. Spain renounced all claim to Cuba, which became independent in 1902. Theodore Roosevelt became a national hero. The war also served to heal many national wounds caused by the Civil War.

James Richard smiled as the information flowed through his head. American History final? Bring it, baby!

"A good apple pie is seventy percent crust," the woman told James Richard's mother. "Can't stress the importance of crust enough. The right amount of cinnamon and sugar, that's another ten percent."

Mrs. McNulty nodded.

"But apples..."

Mrs. McNulty nodded some more.

"Apples is all the rest. Gotta have good apples, young lady."

Mrs. McNulty liked being called a young lady.

"James Richard," she said after the boy dropped out of the tree. "Let's pick a bag of Cortlands."

The old woman smiled her approval. "That's what grandma used," she repeated.

The old couple stayed with the trees while James Richard and his mother made their way back to the dirt road. They sat on a wooden bench. Each ate an apple while they waited for the return of the hay wagon. Behind them, a young man with short brown hair stood holding a half a bag of Sweet Sixteens. Neither Sheila or James Richard knew he was there until they scrambled aboard the hay wagon.

After a brief ride, Peter announced, "Cortland," and James Richard and his mother once again hopped off. The young man with short brown hair stayed aboard. He watched the woman and her son intently until the wagon made a wide turn around a stand of trees, effectively hiding them from view.

James Richard was sure he had seen him before, but couldn't place where.

* * *

"I'm hungry," James Richard announced when they had returned to the entrance of the orchard, each carrying a large bag of hand-picked apples.

"You're always hungry," his mother replied.

How would you know? James Richard almost said. He realized that was unfair though and forced the words back down his throat.

"Food," he said instead, pointing at a small stand set up near the parking lot. The menu featured hot dogs, pop and chips, which was just fine with James Richard. But it also boasted apple cobbler, apple crumble, apple fritters, applesauce brownies, topsy-turvy apple pie and other apple treats that made Mrs. McNulty's mouth water.

"Well," she said. "One must eat." She took James Richard's hand and pulled him so hard toward the stand he nearly lost his balance.

A few minutes later, they were seated alone at a picnic table. Mrs. McNulty had talked James Richard out of hot dogs and pop. Instead, he was eating apple fritters and drinking apple juice and praising both with his mouth full. Mrs. McNulty couldn't bring herself to check her son's manners.

James Richard finished before his mother did and began to look around. He noticed the young man with short brown hair again, this time leaning against the food stand and staring into the distance.

"Hey, Mom. I just remembered where I saw that guy before."

"What guy?"

"The guy over there."

James Richard pointed. The man disappeared behind the stand just as Mrs. McNulty turned around.

"Where?" she asked.

"He just went behind the food stand."

"Who is he?"

"I don't know, but he was hanging around basketball practice yesterday."

"Are you sure?"

"I think so."

They both watched the food stand, but when the man didn't reappear, Mrs. McNulty turned back to her food.

"I wonder where he went?" James Richard asked.

* * *

Sheila McNulty was humming as she drove her Pontiac Grand Am back toward the city. Her voice was light and pretty and James Richard remembered the mother and daughter who sang on the hay wagon. His mother could sing so much better than they did, he thought.

He sighed contentedly, stretched, straining against his seat belt. James Richard loved his mother deeply. He almost told her so. Of course, he didn't. That would have been so uncool. Instead, he glanced out the side passenger window. There was nothing there to hold his attention, so he tried the mirror. He spotted a sky blue car was following behind. In that instant his mind flashed on the blue car that had followed the bus last Thursday night. Lately, that had been happening a lot. James Richard would be thinking of one thing when all of a sudden he would remember something else, something from the bus ride or his visit to the police station: the man with the suitcase, the man who chased him, what the two police officers said in the restroom. Why this was happening? He didn't know, but he didn't believe it was worth asking anyone about. Instead, the boy shook the image out of his head. It couldn't be the same blue car anyway.

The boy turned in his seat and faced his mother.

"What next?" he asked.

She quickly reviewed the activity list in her mind. "The zoo," she said.

"No zoo," James Richard replied, almost contemptuously.

"No zoo?" his mother repeated.

"No way."

"Okay," Mrs. McNulty said, going back over her list. "How about miniature golf?"

"Seriously?"

"Have you ever played miniature golf?"

"Not that I remember."

"Consider it a life experience then."

James Richard shrugged, smiled as his mother exited the highway and hung a left. He glanced at the side mirror again. The blue car was still there. He turned in his seat and looked at it through the rear window. He could not tell who was driving, but a picture of the young man with short brown hair came to mind.

"Mom?" he asked cautiously.

"Hmm?" she asked back.

"Make a right turn."

"What?"

"I think we're being followed. Make a right turn."

Mrs. McNulty glanced up at her rearview mirror; saw the blue car. "Who would follow us?"

"I don't know."

"You're being paranoid," the woman told her son.

"This cop who spoke to the class one time, he said if you think you're being followed you should make three right turns."

"Why?"

"To see if the guy follows you."

"I think you're being silly," she said.

Maybe, James Richard was thinking. He was also afraid. *Maybe it WAS the same blue car that chased the bus.*

"Please, Mom."

"All right."

Sheila McNulty slowed at the next intersection, turned right.

So did the blue car.

"Oh, man," said James Richard. "Oh, man, oh, man, oh, man," he repeated, his voice gaining in intensity with each syllable.

"Stop it, now," his mother urged him. "This doesn't mean anything."

"Turn right again," James Richard told her.

"There's no reason for anyone to be following us."

"Turn right," James Richard repeated.

Mrs. McNulty signaled, slowed, turned right.

The blue car turned with her.

"Oh, man," said James Richard.

"Now you have me worried," Mrs. McNulty told her son, working hard to keep her voice calm. "You said three turns?" James Richard nodded, staring at the reflection of the blue car in the sideview mirror. "Let's be sure," she said.

She turned right at the next intersection.

The blue car drove straight through and disappeared.

"See," said Mrs. McNulty. "Now don't you feel foolish?"

James Richard smiled in return, but no, he didn't feel foolish at all.

* * *

After miniature golf, Sheila McNulty and her son went to a program at the science museum. Next was dinner and a movie, *like a date*, James Richard thought. During the movie, James Richard held his mother's hand and leaned against her shoulder and it was an action picture!

It was approaching midnight when they arrived home. Neither of them noticed the blue car parked on a side street half a block down with a clear view of their house.

EIGHT

A major science exam first thing Monday morning and James Richard figured there ought to be a law against it and by the way they groaned when Miss Hoedeman passed out the four-page test papers, he knew his classmates agreed.

"People, people, people," Miss Hoedeman called out like a carnival barker. "You have forty-five questions and fifty-five minutes to answer them. I suggest you start now."

After a quick glance at the clock above the door, James Richard bent to his task. He had studied most of Sunday afternoon and evening and he was ready. Ignoring the age-old advice of reading all the questions first, he started at the beginning. Page one, question one. He worked quickly and efficiently, shutting out everything around him. He saw nothing except the test. He heard nothing except the scratching sounds his pencil point made on the paper. When he had finished, he looked up at the clock. To his amazement, he still had over twenty minutes left.

"Go back, do it again," his experience told him. He reviewed his answers, changed nothing. He was sure of them all.

* * *

Miss Hoedeman had lobbied for a new classroom every year since she started teaching at St. Rose. It wasn't a bad classroom as classrooms go. It was clean and roomy and had the prerequisite desks and chairs and blackboards. It also had an easterly exposure; for two and a half hours each day the sun pouring through its massive windows was so bright that shades needed to be drawn, giving the room a gloomy, closed-in feeling that Hoedeman hated.

She was at the shades, gripping the cord that would lower them, when she happened to look out the window. On the street, about a block down from the school, a man exited from the driver's side of a blue Ford and stretched his arms toward heaven. A moment later a second man left the car from the passenger side and did the same. The two of them spoke to each other across the roof of the car. As they spoke, a third man poked his head out of a rear window and said something. The first two men shrugged, switched places, and re-entered the car. There they sat.

Miss Hoedeman's mind flipped pages in a handbook she was required to read at the beginning of every school year, stopping at the section that dealt with suspicious persons on and near school property.

"I think this qualifies," she told herself.

She was still wondering about the men in the blue car when James Richard left his seat and walked to the front of the classroom. He set his test papers on her desk. She looked up abruptly at the clock. She hadn't expected anyone to finish much less this early.

Miss Hoedeman left the blinds and returned to her desk. She examined James Richard's papers and after assuring herself that he had answered all the questions, she began to correct them.

* * *

Lacey Mauer was working furiously, yet when the bell sounded, she was only on question forty-two.

"That's it, pencils down" Miss Hoedeman announced. "Hand in your papers as you leave."

Lacey did as she was told, reluctantly. Five more minutes and she would have answered them all, she was sure. She wondered how James Richard had done. She thought she saw him leave his seat midway through the period, probably to ask a question. He was waiting for her at the door.

"Mr. McNulty," Miss Hoedeman called to him just as Lacey reached his side. The seventh graders paused and turned toward her. Miss Hoedeman was holding up James Richard's test paper for him to see. On the top of the page, in a circle, she had drawn a large, bright red A+.

"Welcome back," she said.

The smile on James Richard's face was truly brilliant. Looking at it made Miss Hoedeman smile, too. She was still smiling long after he had left her classroom. To help kids excel and to see their faces when they did was the reason Miss Hoedeman became a teacher in the first place; it's what made all her hard work worthwhile.

She was still smiling when she reached for the telephone on the wall next to the door and called administration to warn them about the three men in the blue car.

* * *

Second period Spanish was taught in a classroom on the first floor, directly beneath the room where they had just taken their science test. Lacey Mauer swung around in her seat to eye James Richard, who sat behind her.

"Did you answer *all* the questions?"

James Richard nodded.

"Hoedeman already corrected your paper?"

James Richard nodded.

79

"And she gave you an A-plus!"

James Richard nodded again, adding a self-satisfied grin.

"If she grades on a curve, I'm going to kill you."

James Richard tried to act frightened, but couldn't quite pull it off. His smile was too broad. He felt just like he had the other day while playing basketball. He was in a zone. He didn't even notice the sun streaming through the windows, causing most of his classmates to squint. But his teacher did.

"Señor McNulty," Miss Spanier called to him. *"Favor de cerrar las cortinas."*

James Richard left his seat and went to the windows to draw the shades. He looked out just as a police car pulled to a stop directly behind a blue car that was parked about a block down from the school. He watched intently as the police officer left his squad car and cautiously approached the driver's door. Just as he reached it, the blue car leapt away from the curb, its rear wheels smoking. The car raced for two blocks and made a hard right, two wheels came off the ground when it did. The police officer retreated quickly to his vehicle. A moment later, it too was screeching away from the curb with siren wailing and lights flashing.

"What's going on?" James Richard asked aloud. Who was in the blue car? Was this the same blue car that followed the bus Thursday night? Or the one that followed him and his mother from the apple orchard Saturday afternoon? Or was this a different blue car altogether? Did this have something to with the money he had found?

The questions came fast and furious but James Richard couldn't answer any of them. He stood watching out the window wondering what to do until Miss Spanier called him back to his seat.

He had stopped smiling.

* * *

Worlie didn't notice as the needle of the speedometer edged past seventy. He was too busy watching the street in front of him. Wind rushed through his open window, whipping his hair. Houses on the residential street blurred until they were only colors passing. Next to him, Truax shouted, "Turn left, turn left!"

Worlie turned. The sound of squealing tires drowned out the radio. The small sedan gained quickly on a mini-van driving the lawful speed. Worlie cut hard left around him. Another van was approaching fast in the oncoming lane. Worlie's heart literally stopped beating. He spun the wheel hard right and pushed fiercely on the gas pedal, just avoiding a head-on collision.

Sickler giggled from the back seat as the Ford rocked back and forth, its suspension not built for this kind of driving.

Truax didn't seem to notice how close to disaster they had come. Instead, he was too busy staring out the back window. "Turn right!" he shouted. Worlie did as he was told. Fear caused him to tap the brakes as he cranked the steering wheel. He drove nearly a half mile at high speed before Truax said, "Right again," then, "keep going straight."

Worlie drove straight. His hands were sweating, but he kept them firmly on the steering wheel.

"Take another right." Truax's voice was dropping in velocity. His breathing was returning to normal. Three blocks later he said, "Take a left. Slow down. You want to get in an accident?"

Worlie slowed to forty miles per hour. He checked his mirror for the police. Nothing. He listened for sirens. He heard at least two, but they were a long way off and moving in the opposite direction.

"Slower," Truax told him.

Worlie reduced his speed to thirty.

"Take another left."

Worlie did, properly this time, signaling well in advance.

Sickler was pressing the back of the seat. He was holding his gun. Worlie saw it out of the corner of his eye.

"What are you doing with that?" he wanted to know.

"What do you think?" Sickler replied.

"You were going to shoot him," Worlie said. "You were going to shoot that cop."

"If I had to," Sickler replied matter-of-factly.

"Oh my God," Worlie said.

"Oh my God is right," Truax added. "You think killing a cop is going to get us any closer to the money, Sickler? Use your head."

Sickler was tired of using his head. He wanted to use his gun. On Truax. It was only the promise of big a payoff that held him back. He settled in his seat. *First the money, then Truax and Worlie,* he told himself silently. Out loud he asked, "Where are we going?"

"There," Truax said, pointing at the parking lot of a shopping mall. "Pull in."

Worlie did what he was told.

"What are we going to do?" he asked.

"Ditch the Ford," Truax said. "By now every cop in the city will be looking for it."

From beneath the front seat, Truax produced a rubber wedge and a "slim jim," a thin strip of metal about eighteen inches long with a hook on the end.

"Any particular color you guys like?" Truax asked as Worlie drove slowly down a long row of parked cars.

Worlie swallowed hard. Now he could add Grand Theft Auto to his crimes.

* * *

James Richard was sitting in his usual spot in the public library, at the table near the floor-to-ceiling windows, his back to the door, his hair still slightly damp from the shower he took following basketball practice. He was listening to rock music, the earbuds of his iPod firmly in his ears, while he studied his math text and wrote equations in a spiral notebook. The music worked as white noise, allowing him to concentrate on his homework. Without it, James Richard would have been distracted by every voice; he would be looking up every time a chair leg scraped against the floor. Unfortunately, it also isolated him from his surroundings. As a result, James Richard didn't see the young man with short brown hair enter the library. He didn't hear when he asked the librarian what time it closed.

NINE

Lacey Mauer didn't even wait until James Richard sat on the bus seat next to her. "Did anyone claim the money?" she asked much too loudly for James Richard's peace of mind.

James Richard said, "No," added, "three days to go."

Lacey squealed her delight, which brought both her and James Richard to the attention of Muchlinski and Landeen, the upperclassmen she had fought the previous year.

"Hey, it's the rich kid," said Muchlinski.

"He's riding the school bus," Landeen noticed. "Hey, rich kid, where's your limousine?"

"Is it the chauffeur's day off?" Muchlinski asked.

On and on it went, Muchlinski and Landeen tormenting James Richard over the five million dollars he had won in the lottery. Like just about everyone else, they had the details wrong. James Richard tried to correct them, but they weren't listening. When Lacey attempted to intervene, the older boys shouted her down.

"This is none of your business, sister," Muchlinski scolded.

"Yeah, sister," added Landeen.

Sister? Lacey thought.

Finally, as the school bus approached St. Rose, James Richard said, "If you don't leave me alone, I'll have my girlfriend beat you up."

My girlfriend.

When Lacey heard the words, her head whipped around so fast to face James Richard that she nearly suffered whiplash.

My girlfriend.

Muchlinski and Landeen, remembering their earlier experience with Lacey, hesitated, then poured it on even heavier than before.

"Need a girl to fight your battles?" asked Muchlinski.

"Sissy boy, sissy boy," Landeen chanted.

James Richard merely smiled. "What do you think, Sally?" he asked.

Sally. He called me Sally. He didn't forget.

"I took 'em once, I can do it again," Lacey replied confidently.

When she left the bus, she handed her backpack to James Richard and went into an American Free Fighting Stance—her favorite karate stance because it gave her greater speed and mobility and because it was just as good for self-defense as it was for offense. Muchlinski and Landeen took one look at her and stepped several feet backward.

"What are you...nuts?" asked Muchlinski.

"Are you crazy?" asked Landeen.

"Can't you take a joke?" said Muchlinski.

"A joke," echoed his friend.

Lacey moved cautiously toward them, keeping her hands high.

"Hey, hey, hey," Muchlinski repeated, moving the same distance backward.

"Hey, hey," said Landeen, joining him.

By now Lacey and the two bullies were surrounded by a crowd of students at least three deep. Some of the kids took up a chant: "Fight, fight." A graceful escape was now impossible. Muchlinski and Landeen were in trouble and they knew it.

"Good morning, students!" a deep voice boomed. Principal Riley was moving among them. "Beautiful day, isn't it?"

In reply, the crowd began to disperse. Lacey abandoned her stance. Muchlinski and Landeen moved close to the tall African-American, seeking his protection.

"Did you see that?" asked Muchlinski.

"She's crazy," said Landeen.

"She tried to pick a fight with us," said Muchlinski.

"She's nuts," said Landeen.

"For no reason at all."

"She's as goofy as a bedbug."

Riley looked down on Landeen, an odd expression on his face. *Goofy as a bedbug? What the heck does that mean?* he wondered.

"McNulty put her up to it," Muchlinski accused.

"Yeah," echoed Landeen. "McNulty paid her."

"She's a paid assassin," said Muchlinski.

"A hit man, woman, person, whatever," agreed Landeen.

Riley turned to face the pretty thirteen-year-old girl. She shrugged and smiled. Behind her James Richard glanced up and down and over and around, taking interest in everything except what was going on directly before him, pretending that he wasn't involved. Riley returned his gaze to Muchlinski and Landeen, noting that they were a foot taller and many pounds heavier than Lacey.

"Did she hurt you?" he asked the boys.

"No, of course not, whaddaya think, we're wimps?" they protested, realizing that their manhood was being questioned.

"You come see me if she does," he told them.

"We can take care of ourselves, we're not afraid of her, she's not so tough," they replied.

Riley used his thumb to point the two boys in the right direction. They quickly hustled to the school building, giving Lacey a wide berth. Riley looked down at the girl.

"Stop picking on the older boys, Mauer," he said.

"Yes, Mr. Riley," she replied sweetly.

Riley glanced at James Richard who was still pretending to be somewhere else. "McNulty," he said.

For the first time, James Richard looked directly at his principal. Only Riley couldn't think of an appropriate warning to give the boy. So he merely shook his head at him and frowned meaningfully before returning to his office.

Lacey was also at a loss for words as she gazed up at James Richard.

He called me his girlfriend.

* * *

The car door opened without warning, making both Truax and Sickler leap in their seats. Sickler's head hit the roof of the car.

"Don't do that!" Truax warned Worlie.

"Do what?" Worlie asked.

"You jerk," said Sickler, rubbing the top of his head.

"What?"

"Never mind," Truax told him. "Did you get it?"

"Yeah," Worlie replied. "He's on bus number fifteen."

"Are you sure?"

"I'm sure."

"That's what he said about Fast Eddie," Sickler reminded everyone.

"Will you stop with that," Worlie demanded. "I said I was sorry."

"You sure are," said Sickler.

Worlie's anger was coming dangerously close to overcoming his fear of Sickler. He was contemplating going over the back seat for his partner's throat when Truax intervened.

"Bus number fifteen?" he asked.

"Yeah," Worlie replied.

"Anybody see you in the parking lot?"

Worlie nodded. "There were a lot of parents dropping kids off and walking little kids to school," he said. "But I don't think anyone noticed me."

"Good."

"Peachy keen," added Sickler.

Truax engaged the ignition with a screwdriver and the engine of the green Ford Taurus sprang to life.

"Let's get out of here," Truax said. The stolen car had been parked three blocks from the school, but Truax wasn't taking any chances. They planned on returning later that afternoon to follow bus number fifteen until it dropped the blond kid at his home.

* * *

He called me his girlfriend.

To say Lacey Mauer was thrilled over the remark would have been a colossal understatement. However, her happiness was tempered somewhat by the end of first period when Miss Hoedeman distributed the corrected science tests from the previous day. James Richard with his perfect paper had received the only perfect score. Lacey had one wrong and three unanswered questions and earned a B-plus.

James Richard patted her on the shoulder and said, "Nice try, Lace."

Lacey was so angry at his smart-aleck remark that she almost decked him right there. Later, she wondered if it was possible to remain James Richard's girlfriend if she got better grades than he did. Would he become jealous? It hadn't been a problem in the past, but they were getting older now. Her pride and competitive spirit silenced the debate. Also, something her father once told her: "If you hide your intelligence so people will like you, one day you'll find that the only people who like you are stupid." She vowed to out-do him the next time around. If he didn't like it, tough!

* * *

Stop and start. Stop and start. Truax was making himself sick as he followed the school bus along its tangled route, dropping kids at their front door. Sickler, too, complained about motion sickness. But complaining wasn't all he did. Opening his window and hanging out in case he threw up. Only Worlie seemed immune, largely because he was too frightened to be sick. For nearly a half hour they had followed the school bus and it had yet to deposit a thirteen-year-old blond kid, any thirteen year-old blond kid, anywhere. He was afraid of what his partners might do to him.

Finally the bus was empty. The driver found a busy thoroughfare and headed for the yard. Truax stopped following. He parked the car and turned in his seat to face Worlie.

"Well, what about it?" Truax asked.

"I don't understand," said Worlie.

"I understand," said Sickler angrily. "You messed up again"

"This is the bus," insisted Worlie. "Bus number fifteen. I'm telling you, it's the right bus."

"You idiot!" screamed Sickler. He followed with a whole lot more insults, most of them laced with obscenities. Worlie lashed back, just as loudly and with equal profanity. Truax, his contempt for his partners at an all-time high, refused to join in. Instead, he stared out the front windshield. He thought that he was working much harder for his share of the armored truck loot than he had expected to. He thought that both of his partners were seriously deranged and the sooner he was rid of them the better. Mostly he thought about the night Fast Eddie stole their money and how the kid came to get his hands on it in the first place.

Truax listened to his partners trade insults and threats until they were out of breath. Finally, he said, "Know something guys, I think we've been going about this all wrong."

* * *

James Richard had been late leaving the library and for a few anxious moments, he was afraid he had missed the bus. Only there it was, bearing down on him, its bright lights offering an inviting refuge against the cool, lonely night.

He boarded, paid his fare and moved toward an empty seat in the back, using the hand railings for support, the bus swaying like the deck of a ship beneath his feet. He had just reached his seat when the bus stopped again. It had traveled only one block. A young man with short brown hair slowly boarded the bus and carefully looked over the dozen passengers until he spotted James Richard. He turned away, found a seat and fixed his gaze out the window. He did not look James Richard's way again.

But James Richard couldn't keep his eyes off of him. It was the man from the gym, he was convinced of it. The same man he had seen at the apple orchard; who had attempted to follow him and his mother.

Who was he?

What did he want?

Why was he following me?

Was it the money?

Questions flooded James Richard's brain, yet no answers were forthcoming.

James Richard's hands began to sweat. He rubbed them on his thighs, partly to dry them and party to keep them from shaking. It was an effort to breathe normally, his pulse rate rose impossibly high.

Maybe the man would get off the bus, James Richard told himself. He prayed that he would. Only with each stop, his prayers went unanswered. James Richard began to fear the man would not leave until he did. Then what?

James Richard's nervousness left his hands and traveled to his legs. Both were quivering. Beads of sweat formed on the back of his neck and under his arms.

Think, think, think, James Richard told himself, tapping his forehead with each *think* like he was Winnie the Pooh. Like the bear, his brain started to feel fluffy. He remembered what the cop said, the one who came to the school and lectured the students about safety. Stay in well-lighted areas. Travel where there were plenty of people. It occurred to James Richard that he was in no danger as long as he remained on the bus. The man wouldn't dare try anything around so many witnesses.

James Richard's confidence increased with that realization. He devised a plan.

It's simple, he told himself. He would signal for his usual stop. If the man rose when he did, James Richard would sit back down. Oops, sorry, made a mistake. If the man sat down, too, then James Richard would know for a fact he was being followed and report it to the bus driver. Tell him that the man was stalking him for some ungodly reason and would he please use his radio to notify the police while he waited right there in the seat next to him. Simple.

Once he had a plan, James Richard began to relax. His legs stopped shaking and his heart beat returned to something close to normal.

Pleased with himself, James Richard waited. The street name changed from University Avenue to Lincoln Parkway and the bright lights of the city gave way to the comparative darkness of the suburb. Miles passed. Finally, his stop loomed ahead of him like a challenge.

With a deep breath and a barely audible, "Here goes," James Richard rose from his seat. He pulled the cord to signal his departure. A sound like a small bell tinkled in the bus driver's ear and he automatically began to slow his speed. James Richard fixed his eyes on the back of the young man's head. The man did not move, did nothing to acknowledge that he knew James Richard was moving.

The bus slowed.

Stopped.

The back door whooshed opened.

James Richard stood at the top step watching the young man.

The young man stayed seated.

James Richard's heart suddenly seemed too big for his chest as he jumped down the steps. The door closed behind him and the bus rumbled on, picking up speed.

James Richard slung his backpack over his shoulders and prepared to run. If the bus even looked like it was going to stop at the next block, he was gone. Fast. The bus did not stop though. James Richard watched as its taillights disappeared from view.

He laughed at himself.

He called himself paranoid.

He jogged happily the entire two blocks to his home.

Two men sitting silently in a dark green Ford Taurus watched his progress with great interest. The one behind the steering wheel took careful note of the address of the huge, white house that James Richard unlocked with a key he wore on a chain around his neck.

"When the time comes, we'll take him here," said Truax under his breath.

TEN

James Richard pushed his lunch tray away. Chicken patty sandwich, shredded lettuce, broccoli and cheese sauce, banana, orange cream bar. How could something that sounded so good on the monthly menu turn out to be so crummy? The chicken was dry, the bun soggy, the lettuce wilted, the broccoli, they didn't actually expect people to eat that stuff did they?

"Two more days," James Richard told himself.

In two days, his mother would be able to quit her night job. Then she would have the time to make his lunch when the school menu called for it, like she did in the days BD—Before Divorce. Thin-sliced, home-cooked turkey on fresh baked bread, her famous corn chowder kept piping hot in a thermos, romaine lettuce and croutons in a plastic container with dressing and grated parmesan cheese on the side, even peanut butter and jelly. James Richard sighed at the thought of it. Well, at least the assembly-line workers who made his lunch now couldn't screw up a banana, he decided. Or could they? He unpeeled it carefully.

"Do you believe this weather?" Lacey asked as she slid into the chair across from him.

"Hmmm," James Richard grunted, his mouth filled with banana.

"Seventy-five degrees, do you believe that? Seventy-five degrees the week before Halloween. I remember when we've had snow on Halloween."

"It can't last," James Richard warned.

"I know it can't last," Lacey said, disgusted at his

pessimism. "That's why we need to enjoy it."

"Hmm," hummed James Richard, his mouth filled with banana.

"You know why we're having such great weather?"

"Hmm?"

"El Nino," Lacey announced. "It's warming the waters of the Pacific Ocean off the coast of South America and that's affecting weather everywhere. Where we are in the Upper Midwest, it means unseasonably warm temperatures," Lacey was quoting the weatherman now, "but everywhere else it means droughts, floods, typhoons tornadoes. I'm going to do my science project on it. I've already started working on mathematical models of weather probabilities around the world."

James Richard shook his head.

"I wouldn't," he said.

"Why not?"

"El Nino? Which is Spanish for 'the child'. Specifically the Christ Child because El Nino usually appears around Christmas; that's why the name is always capitalized? Everybody in school is going to do their project on it."

"Like who?" Lacey wanted to know.

James Richard took another bite of banana in reply.

"You rat," Lacey called him. "Rat, rat, rat, rat, rat." Then, "I suppose we could do the project together."

"I suppose," James Richard said. "You want my broccoli?"

"Ewww," Lacey replied. A moment later she glanced around the cafeteria, lowered her voice and said, "Did, ahh… Did you and your mom hear anything about the money?"

James Richard shook his head.

"No one's claimed it yet?"

James Richard shook his head again.

"Cool."

* * *

No one jumped when Worlie opened the car door this time.

"Well?" asked Sickler.

"He didn't get on the bus after school," Worlie answered.

"Good," said Truax. "He's sticking to his usual pattern."

Sickler studied his watch.

"What'll we do now?" Worlie asked. "Come back at eight-thirty to make sure he takes the city bus?"

"Yes," said Truax.

Sickler was still looking at his watch.

"I wonder what the kid does here for five hours?" he asked no one in particular.

Truax, who was about to use a screwdriver to activate the ignition of the stolen Ford Taurus, stopped and turned toward him.

"Good question," he said. "We'd better find out."

"How?" Sickler asked.

"You go and look."

"What?"

"Go and look."

"Me?"

"Yeah, you."

"Who died and made you king?" Sickler wanted to know.

"It's your turn," Truax insisted.

"No way. I'll let you know when it's my turn for something."

"It's your turn now," Truax told him. "Look in the gym, the library. Try not to be too conspicuous. Don't let him see you if you can avoid it. For God's sake, don't scare him. Just find out what he's doing and then come back. We don't want any surprises tomorrow."

"Why don't you go?" Sickler asked.

"Because if I left you two here alone, someone would likely get shot."

Sickler glanced at Worlie and said, "Since you put it that way." He opened the car door. "You'd better be here when I get back."

* * *

The massive doors at the top of the concrete steps leading to St. Rose of Lima school were locked. So was the side door and the back door. Affixed to the back door was a sign, black with white letters. It read: ALL VISITORS PLEASE REGISTER AT SCHOOL OFFICE.

How am I supposed to do that if I can't even get inside? Sickler thought angrily. He knocked hard on the metal door and peered through the narrow reinforced window that ran the length of the door frame. No one appeared.

So now what?

Sickler's options were limited. He could run around the school, trying all the doors he found, but he didn't want to make the effort. At the same time he didn't want to admit to Truax and Worlie that he couldn't even break into a grade school either. What kind of criminal mastermind would that make him? So he stood staring at the door, *willing* it to open. When that didn't work, he hit it. Then he kicked it. Then he shouted, "Open!" To his utter amazement, it did. A young girl used her back to push it open from the inside while she struggled with a black instrument case that was considerably taller than she was. Sickler was happy to give her a hand, yanking the door so quickly the girl nearly fell. After regaining her balance, she smiled at

Sickler.

"I could have played the violin," she said. "But no. I had to choose the cello."

Sickler merely grunted and turned his face away.

"Gawd, some people's children," the young girl muttered as Sickler disappeared into the school, the door clicking shut behind him.

The first thing Sickler noticed was the video camera aimed at the entrance. He quickly ducked his head and moved down the corridor away from it. After he was sure he was clear, he looked up again. He found another video camera mounted at the end of the corridor aimed right at him.

"What is this, a prison?"

It sure felt that way to Sickler as he moved down the hallway, glancing in one classroom and then the other. He hadn't been inside a school since he dropped out at age sixteen, His feelings about it hadn't changed much though. *School was for suckers,* he told himself. Kids running around in little uniforms saying "Yes sir" and "No ma'am." Teachers constantly telling them what to do, where to go, what to study. Telling them you need a good education if you want a good job, have a good life. Yeah and then making them study stuff they'd never use in their life. Like math. And science. History. As if you had to know who was the sixteenth president of the United States, like you couldn't live without knowing. "It was the guy who came between numbers fifteen and seventeen." That was the answer Sickler once gave a teacher. What did he get for it? Detention. Maybe that's where the kid was, Sickler speculated by the time he reached the staircase at the end of the hall. Detention.

He went up the staircase. On the landing he discovered a plaque attached to the wall. It read:

EXPECTATIONS.
A) Respect Everyone in Words and Actions.
B) Respect Property.
C) Come to Class Prepared and on Time.

Isn't that just like a school? Sickler thought. Always telling people what to do.

He climbed the rest of the way up the staircase. Immediately, he heard the distinctive sound of basketballs being dribbled. *Hey, that's it*, he thought. *Sports. The kid's on a team.* Sickler needed to be sure though. He followed the sound of basketballs until he came to the doorway leading to the gymnasium. He peeked his head inside and saw several young boys in blue shorts and t-shirts with the St. Rose of Lima logo stamped on their chests in red. He didn't see the boy. He was leaning forward to get a better look when he heard a voice behind him.

"Excuse me," the voice said.

Sickler jumped at the sound and pivoted. His hand darted to the gun hidden under his jacket. In front of him was a thirteen-year-old boy with blond hair. Sickler had been blocking his path to the gym.

"It's you!" Sickler blurted.

James Richard backed away. "Me?" he said.

Behind him and across the hall was a door labeled BOYS LOCKER ROOM. He had been changing clothes, Sickler reasoned. That was as far as his brain could take him.

"Ah, ah," Sickler stammered. He remembered Truax's warning: *Don't let him see you. For God's sake, don't scare him.*

"I, ahh…"

"Can I help you?" a second voice asked from behind him.

Sickler turned again. Now he was staring at a man,

100

maybe college age, with the word *Coach* stitched on the pocket of his white knit shirt.

"I was…"

"Are you supposed to be here?" Coach Barczak inquired.

"Yes, I, ah…"

"Where's your button?"

"My button?"

"All visitors are required to wear a button with the school name and the word 'visitor' stamped on it," the coach said.

"Is there a problem here?" asked a third voice.

Sickler turned again. This time he was facing a casually dressed middle-aged man with a two-way radio attached to his belt.

"Ahh…"

"He doesn't have a button," the coach told the man.

"All visitors must report to the school office," the man told Sickler.

"I was, ah, I was looking for it," Sickler said. "I was asking this young man where it was," he added, motioning toward James Richard.

"No, he wasn't," James Richard protested, moving nearer to his basketball coach. "It was like he was looking for me."

"Looking for you?" the man asked.

"That's silly," Sickler assured the trio.

"What do you want here?" the man with the radio asked.

Sickler tried hard, but he couldn't think of a reasonable answer. So he did what he always did when confronted with a difficult situation. He hit the man in the face. As the man fell backward, Sickler pushed the coach hard.

"Hey," yelled Barczak.

Only Sickler wasn't listening. He was running, down

the corridor to the stairs, downs the stairs to the corridor below and out the door. The man with the radio was on his feet now and chasing him. He held the radio in one hand and called into it as he ran.

"What was that all about?" Coach Barczak wanted to know.

James Richard shook his head in bewilderment. Yet even as he did, something cold and hard began clawing at his stomach.

Fear.

It occurred to James Richard then that he had been afraid ever since he found the money in the suitcase.

He wondered if the fear would go away once he had the money.

He doubted it.

ELEVEN

Exactly twenty-six hours later James Richard stood in the corridor separating the gymnasium from the locker rooms. He was leaning against the wall, sweat making his shirt stick to his shoulders and chest.

"I really sucked," he declared.

"What happened?" Lacey asked. She was also drenched in perspiration from practicing basketball with the girls' team.

"I don't know," James Richard answered. "My timing was all off. My passes were either short or too long. My shooting. I think I sank like one basket."

"It's your concentration," Lacey suggested. "Your brain is off somewhere thinking about the money you're going to collect tomorrow."

"I guess," James Richard agreed. "I can't remember a single thing I did in school today."

"Come home with me," his friend suggested. "Instead of studying tonight, come to my house. Take a break."

"Could I?"

"Sure. Meet me here after you shower."

"Is your dad picking you up?"

Lacey shook her head. "He's going to this dinner thing at my mom's law firm. We'll be on our own."

"How are you getting home?" James Richard asked.

"Meghan's mom. She's picking us up."

"Meghan's mom?"

"Uh huh."

"Think she'll mind me tagging along?"

"Naw," said Lacey. "Besides, Meghan likes you."

"She does?"

"That's what she said."

"Really?"

"Yep."

"How come you never told me this before?"

Because I didn't want you to know, Lacey almost answered. Instead, she said, "You never asked."

"Hmm," James Richard hummed. "So Meghan likes me, huh?"

"Meet you here later," Lacey said and walked to the girl's locker room, thinking she should never have brought it up.

* * *

"Wait a minute, wait a minute," Worlie repeated as he pointed out the windshield of the car. "He's leaving."

"What?"

"Look."

It was true. The boy with blond hair was standing next to a red mini-van with two girls. All three were dressed in blue windbreakers with the school name on front and a basketball on the shoulder. A woman came around the van, opened the door and they climbed in.

"What's going on?" Sickler wanted to know.

Truax didn't answer. Instead, he jabbed Worlie in the ribs and said, "Follow that van. Don't even think of losing it."

* * *

The van was easy to follow. The rush hour had pretty much expired and the traffic was not too difficult to negotiate. It was dark enough now to use headlights, but Truax made sure Worlie kept them turned off.

The van took a direct route to the northern suburbs and at first Truax thought it was headed toward the boy's home. But then it turned unexpectedly and drove east for several blocks and then south, picking up the avenue that bordered the Theodore Roosevelt Nature Preserve. The red mini-van followed the avenue for half a mile before stopping in front of a large brick house. Truax forced Worlie to park the car about fifty yards behind the van. He didn't noticed the black SUV that drove past them, stopping fifty yards in front of the van.

***

Meghan waved energetically from the window as the van sped off. James Richard, standing on the boulevard in front of Lacey Mauer's house, waved back.

"I like her," he said.

"She's a jerk," Lacey snipped.

"Why do you say that?"

"Oh, James Richard, you're such a wonderful basketball player," the girl replied in a falsetto tone.

"You're right. What a terrible thing for her to say," James Richard replied.

"You know what I mean."

"Lace, I do believe you're jealous."

Lacey was working up to a response when movement to her right distracted her. A man with short brown hair had stepped out of a car and was walking along the sidewalk toward the two teenagers. James Richard recognized him immediately. He dropped his backpack and grabbed Lacey's hand.

"Wait," the man called as James Richard pulled his friend down the sidewalk away from him.

James Richard did stop. But only because three men were getting out of a dark green car in front of him. One of them was the man he had seen at the gym the night before.

"Don't move!" the man ordered.

"What do you want?" James Richard yelled his question to anyone who cared to respond. When no one did, he turned toward the brown-haired man just in time to see him take a handgun from a holster on his hip.

"Police," he shouted.

Police?

The word bounced against James Richard's brain like a handball. He pivoted back toward the three men. The one he had seen the day before had a gun out, too. He was pointing it at James Richard and Lacey.

"Get down," James Richard screamed. He pulled Lacey to the boulevard; she dropped her backpack and landed next to him

A single gunshot.

It sounded funny to James Richard, more like the crack of a cap pistol than the big booming explosion guns always seemed to make in the movies. Curiosity forced his head up just in time to see the man who had yelled "police" spin and fall backward. James Richard glanced at the three men. They were coming closer. The one with the gun was smiling.

James Richard grabbed Lacey's hand and cried, "Run," before leading her across the street and into the nature preserve.

TWELVE

It was difficult to run while holding onto Lacey's hand and she seemed to be holding back, forcing James Richard to pull her along. Soon though, her speed was matching his. They stopped holding hands and ran with James Richard in the lead and Lacey on his heels. Deeper and deeper into the preserve, dodging trees, ducking under branches, twisting and turning and cutting through the underbrush until finally Lacey said, "Stop."

They sank to their knees. Their breathing was shallow and rapid. They turned to face the direction from which they had come, peering intently into the forest, trying to detect even the slightest movement.

"Who are those men?" Lacey asked when she had gained enough air to speak.

"I don't know."

"They shot that guy. Did you see that? They shot him. Do you think they killed him?"

James Richard nodded, shrugged, shook his head.- He was confused and frightened.

"Was he a cop?" Lacey asked.

"He said he was," James Richard replied, still watching the trail the two of them had blazed through the preserve. "I thought I saw him following me around the last few days, but I don't know."

"The guys who shot him. They weren't cops."

"No."

"They were after you."

"I guess," said James Richard. "I saw one of them

yesterday hanging around the gym. When Coach and I asked him about it, he ran away."

"You think they took off after they shot the cop?" Lacey asked hopefully.

"They want the money."

"Are you sure?"

"What else?"

"Then they're still after us."

"Yes. I figure they're going to kidnap me and force my mom to give them the money." James Richard didn't know where the answer had come from. It just popped into his head. The residue of too much time spent watching TV cop shows probably. Yet he was certain he was right. That meant his mother was also in danger. The realization made him tremble.

Both children were quiet as they began worrying about the trouble they were in. Each reacted to it differently. A few moments ago, James Richard's quick thinking had probably saved them. Now he was unsure and afraid. He couldn't think of what to do. Lacey had panicked during the shooting, freezing like a deer caught in the headlights of a car. Now she was on her home ground, in the nature preserve she knew and understood so well. She felt oddly safe.

A breeze rattled the branches of a tree and she smiled.

"What was that?" James Richard gasped.

"Nothing," Lacey replied. "Listen…"

"What? What do you hear?"

"No, just listen," Lacey urged. "The forest has sounds, natural sounds. The rustle of leaves. Water running through the creek bed. Waves lapping against the lakeshore. The sound wind makes blowing through tall grass. Listen to them. Don't even try to figure out where they're coming from, what's making them. Just listen. It'll only take a little while."

James Richard did what he was told and was surprised to find himself comforted by the noises the forest made. Meanwhile, Lacey looked toward the western sky. The sun would be completely down in just a few moments. It would be dark in the forest. *Good,* she thought. Darkness was her friend. She prayed a silent thank you for the expiration of Daylight Savings Time.

She used the time before the sun dipped below the horizon to study the geography around her and fix their position in the preserve. The small lake with K. G.'s beaver lodge was to the right. The creek snaked from the lake toward them then cut abruptly away to the north. The swamp began several hundred yards in front of her and sprawled to her left. James Richard pulled at her elbow.

"I've listened to the forest," he whispered. "Now what?"

"Now, if you hear anything that wasn't among the sounds you just heard, you'll know it's trouble."

In that instant James Richard heard a loud *crack* off to their right; the sound of a dry twig snapping.

"Like that?" he asked.

Lacey pushed James Richard flat, laid next to him. Her lips were just brushing his ear.

"Don't move," she breathed.

James Richard had no intention of moving. He wasn't sure if it was even possible, if his body would obey him.

The moon had not yet risen, but Lacey shielded both of them with the sleeves of her blue windbreaker so light would not reflect off their faces.

A shuffling of feet through dry leaves. It could have been ten yards off or closer. Lacey wasn't sure and had to fight the temptation to look. The sound stopped; began again, stopped. Lacey and James Richard ceased to breathe. Was it twenty seconds? Thirty? Longer? The sound of feet began to recede until it could be heard no longer.

Lacey breathed quietly into James Richard's ear.

"Get your cellphone," she whispered. "We'll call the police. Then hide here until they come."

"Ahh..."

"What?"

"My cellphone is in my backpack. Where's yours?" The expression on her face gave him his answer. "C'mon. Doesn't anybody use pockets anymore?"

"We'll make for the nature center building," Lacey said. "It's where the naturalists and guides hold their programs, where they have their offices and research facilities. There's bound to be people there. They know me. They'll help us."

James Richard nodded.

"It's a few hundred yards to our left. Follow closely. For God's sake, don't drag your feet."

* * *

"This is impossible," claimed Worlie.

Neither Truax or Sickler paid any attention to him.

They had congregated on the fork in a path they had discovered when they were hiding the police officer's body. One fork led off to the right, the other to the left.

"You go that way," Sickler told Worlie. "I'll go this way. Truax, you stay here. Make sure the kids don't double back and try to get to their house."

Sickler was in charge again. He had just shot a man and the adrenaline pumping through his system was jazzing his senses. He felt energized, felt like he could fly.

"We need to get both of them," he emphasized to his partners. "The kid for the money and the girl so she won't tip the cops until we've left for Canada."

Truax nodded in agreement, even though he no longer had any intention of going to Canada.

Worlie's face was pasty and pale and easily reflected what light the forest had to offer. He looked like he wanted to throw up.

"Don't," Sickler warned him. "We have no time for your Mr. Nice Guy crap. We've got to get those kids and get out of here before someone decides to check up on the cop."

Worlie nodded without enthusiasm. He helped shoot a man and now he was hunting two little kids in the forest. What had he come to?

* * *

James Richard felt they were going awfully slow and told Lacey so.

"Fine," Lacey replied curtly. "You take the lead."

When James Richard didn't move, she squeezed his hand and whispered, "We'll be all right. We're almost there."

Lacey was becoming increasingly doubtful though and alarmed. She could not see the lights of the nature center building and there should be lights. She wondered if she was lost, then shook the thought from her brain. This was *her* nature preserve. She never got lost.

She pushed on until they reached a wide, gravel path. A full moon was rising and the light it cast gave shape to the small, sand-colored stones.

"C'mon, run," Lacey said as she led James Richard down the path. Noise didn't concern her now. They couldn't be more than a hundred yards away from the nature center and safety.

* * *

Sickler moved silently down the narrow dirt trail, peering intently into the black forest as he went. He felt like a kid playing cowboys and Indians. Only this time he carried a real gun instead of a plastic toy. However, a familiar sound cleared his mind of childhood reminisces. He stopped and cocked his ear to the wind. Footsteps. Running. In front of him, further down the path. Sickler began to run, too.

* * *

Lacey couldn't believe it. The nature center was closed. A hand-written note taped to the inside window of the front door told the story:

> *Sorry for the inconvenience. We're closed*
> *for renovations until November 1. Join us*
> *for our pre-Thanksgiving nature programs.*

Lacey pounded hard on the glass. "How could they do that without telling me?"

James Richard couldn't believe the rest of the world hadn't heard her as clearly as he had.

"You expect them to check with you every time they do something?" he whispered back.

Well, yeah, Lacey was thinking as she turned toward James Richard. Her face was bright in the moonlight, her eyes shiny.

"I'm open to suggestions," she said.

* * *

Sickler heard the voices at the same time that the narrow dirt trail broadened into a gravel path. He began to pick up speed, his footsteps making loud crunching sounds on the bits of rock.

* * *

Footsteps running toward them, Lacey heard them first. She thought about the parking lot, maybe a hundred yards down the gravel path from the nature center and rejected it. They would never make it and if they did, they'd be in the open.

Run, her brain told her.

But where?

"Lacey?" James Richard said.

The swamp.

"Follow me," Lacey said, taking James Richard's hand and pulling him away from the building. They ran around the nature center and across the gravel path. James Richard could see the figure of a man running toward them.

"Stop," Sickler ordered, his voice shattering the forest quiet.

Lacey and James Richard ignored him, plunging head-long through the trees and down a long, gently-sloping hill. Lacey was running easily, like she knew where she was going and because of that, James Richard began to relax too, even though he could barely see the trees and branches he only narrowly evaded.

"Over here, over here, over here," Sickler chanted as he plunged into the forest at the same spot. The hill made him nervous. He was afraid of tripping and falling into what? Darkness? He followed anyway. Only he was considerably taller than the children and could not easily avoid the low hanging tree branches that slapped his face and the roots that tangled his feet. Soon the children had disappeared from view. A moment later he was able to hear only the sound of his own labored breathing.

Yet he kept moving forward until he intersected another narrow trail. *Right or left?* he wondered. *No.*

Straight ahead. They had continued running down the hill. He could feel it.

He doubted his feelings only for an instant, when he heard footsteps to his right. Only they were too heavy for the children and they were coming toward him. Sickler watched, his hand tightly gripping the butt of his handgun as a dark figure rounded a bend. It was Worlie.

"They're down there," Sickler said.

"Where?"

Sickler pointed. "Down there."

"What'll we do?"

"You follow them."

"Me?"

"You follow them down the hill. Stay on 'em. Keep 'em moving. I'll circle around. We'll catch them between us."

Worlie didn't think it was much of a plan, but it was better than nothing so he left the trail and carefully picked his way down the hill.

* * *

Truax thought he heard noises behind him: cars, voices, shuffling feet. He quietly followed the path to the edge of the nature preserve, his gun drawn. He looked right, then left. Were all those cars parked along the street before? He couldn't remember. There was no noise and he saw no movement.

His mind was playing tricks on him, he decided.

Truax returned to his lookout post at the point where the path forked and waited. After a few minutes, curiosity got the better of him. He left the path and moved silently to the spot where they had dragged the body of the policeman Sickler had shot.

It was gone.

* * *

Lacey tried to stop when she reached the edge of the swamp, but she had been moving too fast and lost her balance. She flailed both arms, yet it did no good. She was falling into it, afraid less of the water than the noise a splash would make. Only she did not fall. She was startled when a pair of hands gripped her wrist and pulled her away from the edge.

"Thanks," she whispered to James Richard.

"What now?" he asked in reply.

"I know a trail through the swamp," she answered. "Follow me."

James Richard stayed on his friend's heels as they slowly picked their way along the edge of the bog, often grabbing tree branches to keep from sliding in. Finally, they were standing on hard ground.

"It's a very narrow path," Lacey warned. "Step where I step."

Lacey led, James Richard followed, watching her feet, trying to set his in the exact spot she had set hers. The high reeds growing in the marsh came to his arm pits. He brushed them away with his hands, until he realized...

"Lacey, stop."

She turned.

"What?"

James Richard was squatting now, his head below the top of the reeds. Lacey squatted next to him.

"What's wrong?"

"We're exposed. They can see us in the moonlight."

"I didn't think of that," Lacey told him. Fear crept into her voice. "Should we go back?"

"We can't stay here."

"There's a dry spot just ahead," Lacey said. "Big enough for both of us. I sometimes use it for picnics."

"Go," James Richard told her. "Stay low."

Lacey crawled along the path. James Richard followed. Before only their shoes were wet. Now their hands and legs were exposed to the mucky water. James Richard's pants were soaked through to his knees and Lacey's bare legs and the hem of her plaid jumper were streaked with mud. Still, James Richard was surprised at the warmth; it felt like summer water.

Finally, they found the small clearing. They collapsed side-by-side in nervous exhaustion.

"My mother is going to kill me when she sees my clothes," Lacey said.

James Richard figured that was the least of their problems, only he didn't say so. He scrambled to his knees and looked over the tall reeds. He saw nothing and began to breathe easier. The respite was shattered a moment later when he caught movement out of the corner of his eye. He turned toward it.

"What is that?" he whispered excitedly.

Lacey was on her knees beside him.

"An observation platform," she said and then swore bitterly, cutting loose with a long and altogether filthy string of obscenities.

James Richard was stunned. He had never heard Lacey Mauer utter so much as a single curse word in her entire life, not even a biblical "hell." He soon understood her behavior, however.

"It's an observation platform built of wood," Lacey explained. "It gives you a birds-eye view of almost the entire preserve, especially the swamp."

"There's somebody on it," James Richard said, confirming the movement he saw earlier.

"I didn't think," she chastised herself. "I just didn't think."

They both sat down, their backs against the reeds.

"Now what?" James Richard asked.

"Shhhh, I'm thinking," Lacey replied.

His nerves got to him at last and James Richard started to giggle. Lacey told him to stop. James Richard couldn't, but he cupped his hands over his mouth and muffled the sound.

"This isn't funny," Lacey warned him, but his giggling was contagious and after a moment she was laughing, too.

* * *

Worlie slowly made his way along the edge of the swamp. He was well past Lacey's path when he heard voices. *Was someone laughing?* he wondered. He spied Sickler on the observation platform and waved his arms. When that failed to attract his partner's attention, he yelled, "What is that?"

Sickler turned toward Worlie's voice and tried to find him in the darkness. He failed.

"What is that?" Worlie yelled again.

"Get over here," Sickler shouted.

"How?" Worlie asked.

Sickler thought he could see his partner now.

"The swamp is crisscrossed with a half dozen boardwalks," Sickler shouted back. "There's one to your left about a hundred yards. Just follow it."

"Who was making that noise?" Worlie asked again.

"Who do you think?" answered Sickler. "Get over here."

* * *

James Richard and Lacey had stopped laughing.

"I'm sorry," James Richard said contritely. "I couldn't help myself."

"Voices travel a long way over the swamp," Lacey

whispered back. "We need to stay quiet."

"We need to get out of here."

"We can't move," Lacey warned. "If we just stay still and quiet, we'll be safe. They'll never find us out here. It's like with animals. They're practically invisible until they move. It's when they move that they attract the eye."

"You're saying we're trapped out here?"

"No, we're not trapped."

"So what do we do?"

"Wait."

"For how long?"

"Half hour maybe," Lacey said. "Maybe a little longer."

"What happens in a half hour?" James Richard wanted to know.

"The temperature is dropping real fast. Haven't you noticed?"

James Richard hadn't. At least not until Lacey mentioned it. Suddenly, he felt cold.

"What about it?" he asked, snapping the buttons on his wind-breaker to his throat.

"We had a high of seventy-five today, but it's going to drop to thirty-five tonight. When that cold air hits the warm swamp water, this whole park is going to be one huge fog bank. It'll be like walking through a cloud. We'll be able to just get up and go home. They'll never see us."

"Are you sure?" James Richard asked.

Lacey felt insulted. "I've only lived here my whole life," she said.

James Richard folded his legs to his chest and rested his chin on his knees. After a few moments he said, "Know what, Lace? You think pretty good."

THIRTEEN

Sickler didn't understand what was happening. First there were wisps of smoke here and there. A few moments later it was like someone had switched on one of those smoke machines they use at rock concerts. Make that a thousand smoke machines. The entire swamp had disappeared. A short time later, the rest of the nature preserve was gone too. *Was the preserve on fire?* he wondered.

"It's fog," Worlie told him.

Sickler kicked the railing of the observation platform and cursed.

Worlie was smiling. With the moon and stars shining bright above him, the ground-hugging fog reminded him of his first plane ride as a kid. The pilot had taken the airliner above a thunderstorm. Bursting through the last layer of clouds had been almost magical. Suddenly, the plane was surrounded by blue skies and bright sunshine, while below was this angry, billowing floor of menacing gray clouds. A study in contrasts. He had never seen anything so strikingly beautiful.

"C'mon," Sickler grunted.

"Where?" Worlie asked.

"The kid's house. Maybe we can catch him there. We're sure not going to catch him here. Not now. I'm telling you, if I lose that money..."

Worlie followed Sickler down the platform steps and onto the boardwalk. He followed him along the boardwalk through the swamp. With each step he told himself he should run, that he too should try to escape in the fog.

* * *

"After you," James Richard whispered. He could barely see Lacey's head nod in agreement.

"Stay close," she said. "We'll take the path to the boardwalk and then follow the boardwalk to the forest. I know a trail we can use that'll lead us back to my house."

"Sounds like a plan," James Richard agreed.

Only it was more easily said than done. Following Lacey out of the swamp was much more difficult than following her in. Several times he slipped off the path and into the bog. One time he sank into the muck up to his knee. When he pulled his leg out again, his tennis shoe had remained behind.

"Nuts," he said, forgetting himself.

"Be quiet," Lacey hissed.

"Sorry."

"What is it?"

"I lost my shoe."

"Can you get it?"

James Richard pondered the question for a moment. "No," he decided.

"It'll be all right," Lacey told him. "We're almost to the boardwalk."

* * *

Sickler couldn't believe his luck. He had become confused in the fog and had taken the wrong branch. This section of boardwalk went off at a forty-five degree angle from where he wanted to go. He continued anyway, not wanting to get even more lost by attempting to retrace his steps. Now he was hearing voices. He was sure he heard the word, "Nuts."

He stopped. Worlie, who was following behind, walked into his back. "Hey," he said.

"Shhhh," Sickler silenced him.

The two men waited quietly. Somewhere in front of him they heard the light splashing of water followed by a grunt of exertion. A girl spoke softly.

"We're here."

She climbed onto the boardwalk.

Sickler leaned forward.

"Hurry," the girl said.

There, a head bobbing in and out of the fog.

Sickler reached for it.

"What?" the girl cried out.

Sickler's hands tightened around her arms. He drew her to himself. Lacey squirmed and kicked and tried to escape. Sickler pinned her arms to her sides by wrapping his own arms around her.

"Gotcha!" he said.

"Run, James Richard, " Lacey shouted. "Run."

"Stay where you are, James Richard," Sickler called into the night.

"Get away," Lacey screamed.

"Don't move!" Sickler screamed after her.

Lacey's five years of training kicked in. She relaxed her body and quickly reviewed the menu of primary targets: temple, ear, eyes, nose, throat, jaw, collar bone, rib, kidney, spine, solar plexus, groin, knee. Most of them had been eliminated by the way the man held her. But not all. With speed and clarity that surprised even her, Lacey snapped back her head, smashing her attacker's lower jaw with the top of her skull. Then, with her *kiai*, loud shout, ringing in his ears, she stomped hard on his instep with her heel.

The man cried out in pain. Only instead of releasing her, he swung Lacey off her feet high into the air and slammed her body on the boardwalk. Lacey absorbed most of the impact with her shoulder. She lost her breath and groaned pathetically as her body bounced off the wood.

Sickler surveyed the damage to his chin and lower lip. They were both swollen and cut. When he brought his hand away, it was bloody. He looked at the blood with both surprise and anger; a little girl had done this to him. He cursed loudly and yanked the girl to her feet. Her head was cloudy with pain and she was unable to defend herself. Sickler thought about hurting her again, but remembered why he was there. He spun Lacey around and pushed her against Worlie. She would have fallen if Worlie hadn't grabbed her around the waist.

"I am really losing my patience," he shouted.

Lacey felt suddenly ill. Her head was pounding unmercifully and her stomach was doing gymnastics, yet her sense of defiance was still intact.

"Run, James Richard," she screamed with what was left of her strength. Sickler curled his hand into a fist and raised it threateningly. He stepped toward the girl. Lacey turned her face away from the blow. It didn't land. As she turned, Worlie clapped his hand over her mouth.

"She's quiet now," he said.

Sickler grunted angrily and barked, "Keep her that way."

Worlie leaned forward until his mouth was close to Lacey's ear. "Shhhhhh," he hissed gently.

Sickler turned his back and gazed into the fog.

"Come out, come out wherever you are, James Richard," he said.

Although he knelt only a foot away from the edge of the boardwalk, James Richard remained invisible in the fog. He couldn't see what had happened. He didn't know if Lacey had been hurt and spasms of anxiety rippled from one muscle to another, making his entire body shake. He wanted to call out for her, but he was too frightened.

"There's nothing to be afraid of," said Sickler. "I don't want to hurt you or the girl. All I want is my money. It's my money, you know, in the suitcase. Not yours."

Sickler moved forward tentatively. James Richard heard the creak of the boards. He figured the man was maybe five feet away. He tried to make himself smaller.

"It's very simple," Sickler continued. "You come out and then all of us will go to your house. You'll be safe in your house."

James Richard flashed on his mother's face. No, he would not take them to his house, he vowed silently. He would not put her in danger. They could do anything they wanted to him.

"Tomorrow morning your parents go to the cop shop, pick up *my* money, give it to me and then we'll be on our way. No one has to get hurt. What do you say, kid?"

James Richard said nothing.

Sickler waited. His chin throbbed and his foot ached and he decided he had had just about enough of these little brats.

"Are you listening James Richard?"

No reply.

"Okay, how 'bout this? You come out right now or I start working over your girlfriend."

My girlfriend.

Lacey.

"It's all up to you," Sickler continued. "I don't want to hurt her. If something bad happens to her, it'll be all your fault."

Lacey tried to speak to James Richard. Tried to tell him not to give himself up. Only the hand over her mouth turned her shouts into mumbles.

"Okay, if that's the way you want it," Sickler said. "Just remember. It's all your fault." To Worlie he said, "Bring her over here."

Worlie didn't move. He wasn't sure what he was going to do, but he knew he couldn't turn the girl over to Sickler.

"Bring her over here," Sickler insisted.

Worlie was suddenly faced with a decision he had been putting off for years now. It came down to this: was he a *nice* guy or wasn't he? Fortunately for him, he didn't have to answer the question.

"Wait," a voice said.

Sickler turned abruptly.

Before him was a thirteen-year-old boy with blond hair.

"It's you," Sickler said.

"Me," the boy answered.

Sickler raised his hand and slapped James Richard hard across the mouth. James Richard fell. "You've been a lot of trouble," Sickler said. He raised his boot to kick him.

"Wait!" yelled Worlie, still clutching Lacey in his arms. "Don't forget the money."

Sickler smiled and lowered his boot.

"I ain't forgetting nothing," he snarled.

Sickler pulled James Richard to his feet.

"C'mon," he yelled over his shoulder to Worlie and began dragging the boy along the boardwalk, his gun held menacingly in his other hand.

Worlie followed, half-carrying and half-dragging Lacey with him. By the time they reached dry land at the end of the boardwalk, Sickler was hopelessly lost. Too much fog and the unfamiliar terrain had him baffled.

"How do we get out of here?" he asked James Richard, shaking him roughly.

"I don't know," James Richard replied honestly.

Sickler turned toward Lacey. "Tell me," he said.

When she hesitated, he raised his gun and prepared to whip James Richard in the face with the barrel. "Just remember, it's all your fault," he said.

"That way," Lacey said despairingly, pointing down the path.

Sickler smiled a sick smile of triumph and pulled James Richard in the direction Lacey had pointed. With Lacey as guide, it wasn't long before they escaped the fog and climbed the hill, rejoining Truax at the fork of the path just below Lacey's home.

"You got 'em?" Truax asked.

"We got 'em," Sickler confirmed.

"It took you long enough."

"Who asked you?"

"We've got to get out of here," Truax warned.

"What do you mean 'we'," Sickler asked, raising his gun. He pointed it at the center of Truax's chest.

Truax reached for his own gun and was quick enough to wrestle it from his pocket. He knew it was a wasted gesture. In the split second before Sickler squeezed the trigger Truax cursed himself for not killing his killer when he had the chance.

***

Lacey screamed in horror. She watched as the bullets ripped the man's body. Watched as he fell backwards, his arms raised to heaven. Watched him hit the ground, bounced slightly, then became still, a bloody red stain growing larger across his chest. Nothing in her life had prepared her for such a callous and heinous act. Not movies. Not TV. Not video games. This was real. A director wasn't going to yell "cut." The man wasn't going get off the ground and go out for pizza with his friends. A man had been killed. A precious human life had been wasted. The man who killed him took away everything he had or was ever going to have. At the same time he hurt every person who knew his victim, who liked him, who cared for him, who gave him birth and raised him. It was terrible, rotten, brutal, lousy thing to do and having seen it Lacey knew she would never be the same person again.

She slowly collapsed to her knees and folded her body until her forehead rested against the cool, damp ground. She heard herself calling for her mother and father, calling for someone she loved and who loved her to explain it all away, only they were not there. Lacey looked for James Richard and found him still in Sickler's grip, staring down at the dead body. His face was chalky white and his dark eyes held an almost unbearable pain.

"Oh God, oh Jesus, oh man," Worlie sputtered. "Why? Why did you...? Oh God."

Sickler pointed his gun at him. Worlie begged, "Please, please don't, please..."

"Shut up," Sickler ordered. "Get the girl up, get 'er moving."

Worlie bent over the young girl. "C'mon, sweetie," he said. There was no comfort in his voice. Only fear. He reached for the girl in the darkness, but instead of touching her, his fingers found a gun. Truax's gun! It had flown from his hand as the bullet tore through his chest. Worlie picked it up and slid it unseen into his own pocket.

With some effort he managed to get Lacey to her feet and followed Sickler past the remaining trees and into the light cast by the street lamps that lined the avenue separating the preserve from the outside world. They halted for a moment at the curb, then Sickler propelled James Richard toward the dark green Ford Taurus, his fingers tightly gripping the collars of boy's shirt and wind-breaker.

They never made it.

Just as the foursome reached the center of the well-lit street, a dozen police officers appeared, popping up from behind parked cars, coming out from behind trees.

"Police! Don't move!" a voice screamed.

All the police officers were holding guns. They were pointing the guns at Sickler and Worlie.

"This is as far as it goes," an officer called from behind the Taurus. "Drop your guns."

James Richard recognized him as the sergeant from the police department, the one who had taken such an interest in his mother.

Sickler pulled James Richard closer, taking what protection he could from the boy's body. He pressed the barrel of his gun against James Richard's temple.

"Drop my gun? Drop your guns!"

"It's not going to happen!" the sergeant shouted back.

"Drop them or I'll kill the boy!"

"All right, boys," Rustovich called.

Sickler was so happy at his new-found power, he didn't even notice that the police officers lowered their guns but *did not* drop them as they were instructed.

"Get in the car, Worlie," Sickler called over his shoulder. "You drive."

Worlie had been standing behind Sickler. He had not moved a muscle since the police appeared. He was almost happy to see them. It meant he didn't need to confront his feelings over what Sickler was doing. Someone else was deciding the course of his life. But that ended with Sickler's command. Now he was forced to make his own decision, one he had just barely avoided making a few minutes earlier—exactly what kind of human being was he? What kind of person did he want to be?

He made that decision in a surprisingly short period of time.

Worlie bent low enough to whisper into Lacey Mauer's ear. He pointed her at the police officers standing behind them. One of them was the officer who had been shot earlier, his left shoulder wrapped in a bandage; apparently he had refused to leave the scene.

"Go to them, sweetie," Worlie whispered. This time there was not even a spark of fear in his voice.

Lacey looked into this eyes. She was afraid it was some kind of trick.

Worlie smiled sadly. "It's all right," he whispered. "Go on."

Lacey raced across the street.

Sickler was growing impatient. He wondered what was keeping Worlie. He turned just in time to see the girl run off. "What are you doing?" he asked.

"It's over," Worlie answered quietly.

"It's over when I say it's over," Sickler assured him.

Worlie shook his head.

Sickler tightened his grip on James Richard.

"I'm getting out of here and the kid's coming with me," he vowed. "No one is gonna…"

He stopped talking when he felt the muzzle of a handgun pressed against the base of his neck.

"No," Worlie said softly.

Sickler smiled his odd, sick smile.

"You wouldn't shoot me," he said. "You're a nice guy. Nice guys don't shoot people."

Worlie thumbed back the hammer of the handgun. The noise it made sent shivers through Sickler's body.

"I stopped being a nice guy the day I started to steal," he said.

Sickler tossed his gun to the pavement.

* * *

James Richard and Lacey were huddled close together on a bench at the police building. James Richard had his arms wrapped around Lacey. Lacey was crying. She had been crying for nearly an hour and had been unable to stop. A call had been placed to her parents, but they had not yet arrived.

A call had also been made to James Richard's mother, who thought there must be some mistake. Her son, and Lacey Mauer, somehow involved with thieves and killers? What nonsense.

She was the first to arrive, sweeping through the building like a high wind, ignoring everyone and everything as she made her way to James Richard's side. James Richard had not cried throughout the ordeal. Yet when he saw his beautiful mother rushing toward him, the tears began to flow.

"Are you all right, are you hurt, what happened?" she asked.

James Richard could answer none of his mother's questions. When she wrapped her arms around him, he laid his head against her chest and wept.

Sheila McNulty held him close. At the same time, she reached for Lacey and pulled her close, too.

They sat like that for a long time.

* * *

When the explanations finally came, Sheila McNulty and Mr. and Mrs. Mauer could only listen with their mouths hanging open, utterly shocked.

Lieutenant Kennedy told them that he knew that the money James Richard found in the suitcase came from the armored truck robbery. He knew that Sickler, Truax and Worlie had beaten Fast Eddie Meeks when Eddie had tried to steal it from them. And he knew that they would try to take it from James Richard. That's why he had a detective—the man with short brown hair—following James Richard, watching over him. The police had set a trap. As soon as the thieves tried to grab James Richard, they were going to swoop down and arrest them. Only the plan backfired when James Richard went home with Lacey Mauer instead of taking the city bus.

"Still," the police lieutenant said. "Your children were very brave. Without them we would never have caught these men."

Kennedy was smiling when Sheila McNulty rose to her feet.

Her voice started low and slowly built into a scream.

"Do you mean to tell us that you used our children for bait?"

EPILOGUE

On Saturday evening they gave Lieutenant Michael Kennedy a retirement party. Every member of the police department not on duty was present. So was the mayor, members of the city council, the county attorney and dozens of other dignitaries. Kennedy had been expected to make a speech summing up his thirty years with the police department. He had spent weeks writing it and rehearsing it. But the speech was canceled. Instead he spent only thirty seconds in front of the microphone, just enough time to thank everyone for coming. His broken teeth had made it too difficult for him to speak.

* * *

"How's your wrist?" James Richard asked.

Sheila McNulty flexed her hand slightly. She had badly sprained her wrist when she punched the police lieutenant and it was wrapped in an elastic bandage.

"It hurts," Mrs. McNulty answered.

"You should have Lacey teach you how to throw a punch," James Richard suggested.

Mrs. McNulty smiled. "I really like that girl," she said.

"Yeah, so do I."

James Richard was sitting on the edge of a sofa. Mrs. McNulty motioned for him to give her room so she could sit next to him.

"We need to talk," she said. James Richard nodded. "Lost in the events of the last two days was a little good

131

news. I was given a promotion, Thursday..."

"Really? That's super," James Richard said, happy for his mother. "We are talking about your daytime job?"

"Yes, dear. I am now a vice president in charge of the entire accounting department."

"Excellent."

"It also means a raise."

"Really, really excellent."

"Yes, it is. But not so excellent that we can keep this up."

"Keep what up?"

"The big house, the cars, all this stuff," Mrs. McNulty said, waving at her living room. "I don't want to work nights anymore. I want to be here for you; I want to spend as much time with you as I can."

Tears began to well up in James Richard's eyes. He turned away and brushed them out of his eyes before turning back to his mother. He had done enough weeping to last a lifetime, he had decided.

"I think we should sell the house and get something smaller," Mrs. McNulty added. "Smaller and less expensive."

James Richard agreed.

"We only need one car, at least until you're old enough to drive. Oh, there are a lot of other things we can do without."

"I could get a job," James Richard volunteered. "That way you won't have to buy my computer programs and stuff."

"Yes, you could," said Mrs. McNulty. "But only if it doesn't interfere with your school work. We are going to get you back on the A honor roll, young man."

"Will I stay at St. Rose?" James Richard asked cautiously.

"Absolutely."

James Richard hugged his mother.

"We'll be all right," she told him. "We're going to be fine."

"It's too bad about the money though," James Richard said. "It's too bad they made us give it back."

"It belongs to the insurance company," his mother reminded him. "Quite frankly, I'm glad. That money has caused us enough problems."

Mrs. McNulty would have said more, but a knock on her front door interrupted her. On her doorstep she found an officious looking man carrying a small briefcase. The man identified himself as an agent for North American Insurance Company and after promising that he was not selling policies, Mrs. McNulty allowed him to enter her house.

"I will not take up too much of your time," the man promised. When he saw James Richard he smiled broadly. "Ah, the brave lad." He shook the boy's hand. "A pleasure to meet you."

"Thanks," said James Richard, who was about as confused as he ever hoped to be.

"As you know, the four hundred and sixty-eight thousand dollars you recovered belonged to North American Insurance Company," the agent said. "It is the amount we paid to cover the losses from the unfortunate armored truck robbery of six months earlier. We at NAIC are grateful, of course, for the return of our property. While NAIC has no written policy covering such occurrences, we at NAIC, and the Total Security Armored Truck Company concurs, would like to demonstrate our appreciation by presenting to you this check representing a percentage of the value of the recovered property. Call it a finder's fee, if you will."

He handed a check to James Richard, whose eyes popped as he read the figure. The boy passed it to his mother. Her eyes popped a little, too.

"For tax purposes, we made out the check to your son, Mrs. McNulty," the insurance agent said. "I hope you approve."

"I do indeed," said Mrs. McNulty.

"That concludes our business," the agent said. "It was a pleasure meeting you both."

Mrs. McNulty led him to the door. When she returned, she found James Richard staring at the check.

"A fifteen percent finder's fee—seventy thousand, two hundred dollars," she said. "That's a lot of money."

"Yes it is," James Richard agreed.

"What are you going to buy with it?"

James Richard lifted his eyes from the paper and smiled at his mother.

"Truth is," he said. "I already have everything I need."

ABOUT THE AUTHOR

David Housewright is an Edgar Award-winning author of the Rushmore McKenzie and Holland Taylor novels as well as other tales of murder and mayhem. He has written 14 books including Penance (1996 Edgar Award winner and Shamus nominee), Practice to Deceive (1998 Minnesota Book Award winner), Dearly Departed, A Hard Ticket Home, Tin City (2006 Minnesota Book Award nominee), Pretty Girl Gone, Dead Boyfriends, Madman On A Drum, Jelly's Gold (2010 Minnesota Book Award winner), The Taking of Libbie, SD (2011 Minnesota Book Award nominee), Highway 61, The Devil and the Diva (with Renee Valois) and Curse of the Jade Lily. His short stories have appeared in numerous anthologies and publications.

OTHER TITLES FROM DOWN AND OUT BOOKS

By J.L. Abramo
Catching Water in a Net
Clutching at Straws
Counting to Infinity
Gravesend

By Trey R. Barker
2,000 Miles to Open Road
Road Gig: A Novella
Exit Blood (*)

By Richard Barre
The Innocents
Bearing Secrets
Christmas Stories
The Ghosts of Morning
Blackheart Highway
Burning Moon
Echo Bay (*)

By Milton T. Burton
Texas Noir

By Reed Farrel Coleman
The Brooklyn Rules

By Don Herron
Willeford (*)

By Terry Holland
An Ice Cold Paradise
Chicago Shiver
Warm Hands, Cold Heart (*)

By Valester Jones
The Pimp and the Gangster (*)

By Bill Moody
Czechmate
Fair Trade (*)

By Gary Phillips
The Perpetrators
Scoundrels (Editor)

By Lono Waiwaiole
Wiley's Lament
Wiley's Shuffle
Wiley's Refrain
Dark Paradise

(*)—Coming in 2012

CPSIA information can be obtained at www.ICGtesting.com
Printed in the USA
BVOW05s2135080815

412476BV00001B/8/P

9 781937 495398